4 2012

MW00780627

MIRA GRANT

This special signed edition is
limited to 1000 numbered copies.

∞

This is copy 576.

WHEN WILL YOU RISE:
Stories to End the World

WHEN WILL YOU RISE:

Stories to End the World

∞

MIRA GRANT

SUBTERRANEAN PRESS 2012

First Edition

ISBN
978-1-59606-462-1

Subterranean Press
PO Box 190106
Burton, MI 48519

www.subterraneanpress.com

TABLE OF CONTENTS

COUNTDOWN

8

"The Rising is ultimately a story of humanity at both its very best, and at its very worst. If a single event were needed to represent all of human history, we could do worse than selecting the Rising." –Mahir Gowda

"People blame science. Shit, man, people shouldn't blame science. People should blame people." –Shaun Mason

May 15, 2014: Denver, Colorado.

How are you feeling today, Amanda?" Dr. Wells checked the readout on the blood pressure monitor, his attention only half on his bored-looking teenage patient. This was old hat by now, to the both of them. "Any pain, weakness, unexplained bleeding, blurriness of vision…?"

"Nope. All systems normal, no danger signs here." Amanda Amberlee let her head loll back, staring up at the colorful mural of clouds and balloons that covered most of the ceiling. She remembered when the staff had painted that for her. She'd been thirteen, and they'd wanted her to feel at ease as they pumped her veins full of a deadly disease designed to kill the disease that was already inside her. "Are we almost done? I have a fitting to get to."

"Ah." Dr. Wells, who had two teenage girls of his own, smiled. "Prom?"

"Prom," Amanda confirmed.

"I'll see what I can do." Dr. Wells took impatience and surliness as insults from most patients. Amanda was a special case. When he'd first started treating her, her leukemia had been so advanced that she had no energy for complaining or talking back. She'd submitted to every test and examination willingly, although she had a tendency to fall asleep in the middle of them. From her, every snippy comment and teenage eye-roll was a miracle, one that could be attributed entirely to science.

Marburg EX19—what the published studies were starting to refer to as "Marburg Amberlee," after the index case, rather than "Marburg Denver," which implied an outbreak and would be bad for tourism— was that miracle. The first effective cancer cure in the world, tailored from one of the most destructive viruses known to man. At thirteen, Amanda Amberlee had been given at most six months to live. Now, at eighteen, she was going to live to see her grandchildren... and none of them would ever need to be afraid of cancer. Like smallpox before it, cancer was on the verge of extinction.

Amanda lifted her head to watch him draw blood from the crook of her elbow. Any fear of needles she may have had as a child had died during the course of her cancer treatments. "How's my virus doing?" she asked.

"I haven't tested this sample yet, but if it's anything like the last one, your virus should be fat and sleepy. It'll be entirely dormant within another year." Dr. Wells gave her an encouraging look. "After that, I'll only need to see you every six months."

"Not to seem ungrateful or anything, but that'll be awesome." The kids at her high school had mostly stopped calling her "bubble girl" once she was healthy enough to join the soccer team, but the twice-monthly appointments were a real drain on her social calendar.

"I understand." Dr. Wells withdrew the needle, taping a piece of gauze down over the small puncture. Only a drop of blood managed to escape. "All done. And have a wonderful time at prom."

Amanda slid out of the chair, stretching the kinks out of her back and legs. "Thanks, Dr. Wells. I'll see you in two weeks."

Daniel Wells smiled as he watched the girl who might well represent the future of mankind walk out of his office. A world without cancer. What a beautiful thing that would be.

—

Dr. Daniel Wells of the Colorado Cancer Research Center admitted in an interview this week that he was "guardedly optimistic" about having a universal cure for cancer by the end of the decade. His protocol was approved for human testing five years ago, and thus far, all subjects have shown improvement in their conditions...

May 15, 2014: Reston, Virginia.

The misters nested in the ceiling above the feeding cages went off promptly at three, filling the air in the hot room with an aerosolized mixture of water and six different strains of rhinovirus. The feeding cages were full of rhesus monkeys and guinea pigs that had entered five minutes earlier, when the food was poured. They ignored the thin mist drifting down on them, their attention remaining focused entirely on the food. Dr. Alexander Kellis watched them eat, making notes on his iPad with quick swipes of his index finger. He didn't look down.

"How's it looking?"

"This is their seventh exposure. So far, none of them have shown any symptoms. Appetites are good, eyes are clear; no runny noses, no coughing. There was some sneezing, but it appears that Subject 11c has allergies."

The man standing next to America's premier expert in genetically engineered rhino- and coronaviruses raised an eyebrow. "Allergies?"

"Yes." Dr. Kellis indicated one of the rhesus monkeys. She was sitting on her haunches, shoving grapes into her mouth with single-minded dedication to the task of eating as many of them as possible before one of the other monkeys took them away. "I'm pretty sure that she's allergic to guinea pigs, poor thing."

His companion laughed. "Yes, poor thing," he agreed, before leaning in and kissing Dr. Kellis on the cheek. "As you may recall, you gave me permission yesterday to demand that you leave the lab for lunch. I have a note. Signed and everything."

"John, I really—"

"You also gave me permission to make you sleep on the couch for the rest of the month if you turned me down for anything short of one of the animals getting sick, and you know what that does to your back." John Kellis stepped back, folding his arms and looking levelly at his husband. "Now which is it going to be? A lovely lunch and continued marital bliss, or night after night with that broken spring digging into your side, wishing you'd been willing to listen to me when you had the chance?"

Alexander sighed. "You don't play fair."

"You haven't left this lab during the day for almost a month," John countered. "How is wanting you to be healthy not playing fair? As funny as it would be if you got sick while you were trying to save mankind from the tyranny of the flu, it would make you crazy, and you know it."

"You're right."

"At last the genius starts to comprehend the text. Now put down that computer and get your coat. The world can stay unsaved for a few more hours while we get something nutritious into you that didn't come out of a vending machine."

This time, Alexander smiled. John smiled back. It was reflex, and relief, and love, all tangled up together. It was impossible for him to look at that smile and not remember why he'd fallen in love in the first place, and why he'd been willing to spend the last ten years of his life with this wonderful, magical, infuriating man.

"We're going to be famous for what we're doing here, you know," Alexander said. "People are going to remember the name 'Kellis' forever."

"Won't that be a nice thing to remember you by after you've died of starvation?" John took his arm firmly. "Come along, genius. I'd like to have you to myself for a little while before you go down in history as the savior of mankind."

Behind them in the hot room, the misters went off again, and the monkeys shrieked.

—

Dr. Alexander Kellis called a private press confer-ence yesterday to announce the latest developments in his oft-maligned "fight against the common cold." Dr. Kellis holds multiple degrees in virology and molecular biology, and has been focusing his efforts on prevention for the past decade...

May 29, 2014: Denver, Colorado.

D r. Wells? Are you all right?"

Daniel Wells turned to his administrative assistant, smiling wanly. "This was supposed to be Amanda's follow-up appointment," he said. "She was going to tell me about her prom."

"I know." Janice Barton held out his coat. "It's time to go."

"I know." He took the coat, shaking his head. "She was so young."

"At least she died quickly, and she died knowing she had five more years because of you."

Between them, unsaid: and at least the Marburg didn't kill her. Marburg Amberlee was a helper of man, not an enemy.

"Yes." He sighed. "All right. Let's go. The funeral begins in half an hour."

MIRA GRANT

—

Amanda Amberlee, age eighteen, was killed in an automobile accident following the Lost Pines Senior Prom. It is believed the driver of the car had been drinking...

June 9, 2014: Manhattan, New York.

The video clip of Dr. Kellis's press conference was grainy, largely due to it having been recorded on a cellular phone—and not, Robert Stalnaker noted with a scowl, one of the better models. Not that it mattered on anything more than a cosmetic level; Dr. Kellis's pompous, self-aggrandizing speech had been captured in its entirety. "Intellectual mumbo-jumbo" was how Robert had described the speech after the first time he heard it, and how he'd characterized it yet again while he was talking to his editor about taking this little nugget of second-string news and turning it into a real story.

"This guy thinks he can eat textbooks and shit miracles," was the pitch. "He doesn't want people to understand what he's really talking about, because he knows America would be pissed off if he spoke English long enough to tell us how we're all about to get screwed." It was pure bullshit, designed to prey on a fear of science. And just as he'd expected, his editor jumped at it.

The instructions were simple: no libel, no direct insults, nothing that was already known to be provably untrue. Insinuation, interpretation, and questioning the science were all perfectly fine, and might turn a relatively uninteresting story into something that would actually sell a few papers. In today's world, whatever sold a few papers was worth pursuing. Bloggers and internet news were cutting far, far too deeply into the paper's already weak profit margin.

"Time to do my part to fix that," muttered Stalnaker, and started the video again.

He struck gold on the fifth viewing. Pausing the clip, he wound it back six seconds and hit "play." Dr. Kellis's scratchy voice resumed, saying, "—distribution channels will need to be sorted out before we can go beyond basic lab testing, but so far, all results have been—"

Rewind. Again. "—distribution channels—"

Rewind. Again. "—distribution—"

Robert Stalnaker smiled.

Half an hour later, his research had confirmed that no standard insurance program in the country would cover a non-vaccination preventative measure (and Dr. Kellis had been very firm about stating that his "cure" was *not* a vaccination). Even most of the upper-level insurance policies would balk at adding a new treatment for something considered to be of little concern to the average citizen—not to mention the money that

Countdown

the big pharmaceutical companies stood to lose if a true cure for the common cold were actually distributed at a reasonable cost to the common man. Insurance companies and drug companies went hand-in-hand so far as he was concerned, and neither was going to do anything to undermine the other.

This was all a scam. A big, disgusting, money-grubbing scam. Even if the science was good, even if the "cure" did exactly what its arrogant geek-boy creator said it did, who would get it? The rich and the powerful, the ones who didn't need to worry about losing their jobs if the kids brought home the sniffles from school. The ones who could afford the immune boosters and ground-up rhino dick or whatever else was the hot new thing right now, so that they'd never get sick in the *first* place. Sure, Dr. Kellis never *said* that, but Stalnaker was a journalist. He knew how to read between the lines.

Robert Stalnaker put his hands to the keys and prepared to make the news.

—

Robert Stalnaker's stirring editorial on the stranglehold of the rich on public health met with criticism from the medical establishment, who called it "irresponsible" and "sensationalist." Mr. Stalnaker has yet to reply to their comments, but has been heard to say, in response to a similar but unrelated issue, that the story can speak for itself...

June 11, 2014:
Allentown, Pennsylvania.

Hazel Allen was well and truly baked. Not just a little buzzed, oh, no; she was baked like a cake. The fact that this rhymed delighted her, and she started to giggle, listing slowly over to one side until her head landed against her boyfriend's shoulder with a soft "bonk."

Brandon Majors, self-proclaimed savior of mankind, ignored his pharmaceutically impaired girlfriend. He was too busy explaining to a rapt (and only slightly less stoned) audience exactly how it was that they, the Mayday Army, were going to bring down The Man, humble him before the masses and rise up as the guiding light of a new generation of enlightened, compassionate, totally bitchin' human beings.

Had anyone bothered to ask Brandon what he thought of the idea that one day, the meek would inherit the Earth, he would have been completely unable to see the irony.

"Greed is the real disease killing this country," he said, slamming his fist against his own leg to punctuate his statement. Nods and muttered statements of agreement rose up from the others in the room (although not from Hazel, who was busy trying to braid her fingers together). "Man, we've got so much science and so many natural resources, you think anybody should be hungry? You think anybody should be homeless? You think anybody should be eating animals? We should be eating genetically engineered magic fruit that tastes like anything you want, because we're supposed to be the *dominant species*."

"Like Willy Wonka and the snotberries?" asked one of the men, sounding perplexed. He was a bio-chem graduate student; he'd come to the meeting because he'd heard there would be good weed. No one had mentioned anything about a political tirade from a man who thought metaphors were like cocktails: better when mixed thoroughly.

"Snozberries," corrected Hazel dreamily.

Brandon barely noticed the exchange. "And now they're saying that there's a *cure* for the *common cold*. Only you know who's going to get it? Not me. Not you. Not our parents. Not our kids. Only the people who can *afford* it. Paris Hilton's never going to have the sniffles again, but you and me and everybody we care about, we're screwed. Just like everybody who hasn't been working for The Man since this current corrupt society

came to power. It's time to change that! It's time to take the future out of the hands of The Man and put it back where it belongs—in the hands of the people!"

General cheering greeted this proclamation. Hazel, remembering her cue even through the haze of pot smoke and drowsiness, sat up and asked, "But how are we going to do that?"

"We're going to break in to that government-funded money-machine of a lab, and we're going to give the people of the world what's rightfully theirs." Brandon smiled, pushing Hazel gently away from him as he stood. "We're going to drive to Virginia, and we're going to snatch that cure right out from under the establishment's nose. And then we're going to give it to the world, the way it should have been handled in the first place! Who's with me?"

Any misgivings that might have been present in the room were overcome by the lingering marijuana smoke and the overwhelming feeling of revolution. They were going to change the world! They were going to save mankind!

They were going to Virginia.

—

A statement was issued today by a group calling themselves "The Mayday Army," taking credit for the break-in at the lab of Dr. Alexander Kellis. Dr. Kellis, a virologist working with genetically tailored diseases, recently revealed that he was working on a cure for the common cold, although he was not yet at the stage of human trials...

June 11, 2014: Berkeley, California.

Phillip! Time to come in for lunch!" Stacy Mason stood framed by the back door of their little Berkeley professor's home (soon to be fully paid-off, and wouldn't that be a day for the record books?), wiping her hands with a dishrag and scanning the yard for her wayward son. Phillip didn't mean to be naughty, not exactly, but he had the attention span of a small boy, which was to say, not much of an attention span at all. *"Phillip!"*

Giggling from the fence alerted her to his location. With a sigh that was half-love, half-exasperation, Stacy turned to toss the dishrag onto the counter before heading out into the yard. "Where are you, Mister Man?" she called.

More giggling. She pushed through the tall tomato plants—noting idly that they needed to be watered before the weekend if they wanted to have any fruit before the end of the month—and found her son squatting in the

29

middle of the baby lettuce, laughing as one of the Golden Retrievers from next door calmly washed his face with her tongue. Stacy stopped, biting back her own laughter at the scene.

"A conspiracy of misbehavior is what we're facing here," she said.

Phillip turned to face her, all grins, and said, "Ma!"

Stacy nodded obligingly. Phillip was a late talker. The doctors had been assuring her for over a year that he was still within the normal range for a boy his age. Privately, she was becoming less and less sure—but she was also becoming less and less certain that it mattered. Phillip was Phillip, and she'd love him regardless. "Yes."

"Oggie!"

"Again, yes. Hello, Marigold. Shouldn't you be in your own yard?"

The Golden Retriever thumped her tail sheepishly against the dirt, as if to say that yes, she was a very naughty dog, but in her defense, there had been a small boy with a face in need of washing.

Stacy sighed, shaking her head in good-natured exasperation. She'd talked to the Connors family about their dogs dozens of times, and they tried, but Marigold and Maize simply refused to be confined by any fence or gate that either family had been able to put together. It would have been more of a problem if they hadn't been such sweet, sweet dogs. Since both Marigold and her brother adored Phillip, it was more like having convenient canine babysitters right next door. She just wished they wouldn't make their unscheduled visits so reliably at lunchtime.

"All right, you. Phillip, it's time for lunch. Time to say good-bye to Marigold."

Phillip nodded before turning and throwing his arms around Marigold's neck, burying his face in her fur. His voice, muffled but audible, said, "Bye-time, oggie." Marigold wuffed once, for all the world like she was accepting his farewell. Duty thus done, Phillip let her go, stood, and ran to his mother, who caught him in a sweeping hug that left streaks of mud on the front of her cotton shirt. "Ma!"

"I just can't get one past you today, can I?" she asked, and kissed his cheek noisily, making him giggle. "You go home now, Marigold. Your people are going to worry. Go home!"

Tail wagging amiably, the Golden Retriever stood and went trotting off down the side yard. She probably had another loose board there somewhere; something to have Michael fix when he got home from school and could be sweet-talked into doing his share of the garden chores. In the meanwhile, the dogs weren't hurting anything, and Phillip *did* love them.

"Come on, Mister Man. Let's go fill you up with peanut butter and jelly, shall we?" She kissed him again before putting him down. His giggles provided sweet accompaniment to their walk back to the house. Maybe it was time to talk about getting him a dog of his own.

Maybe when he was older.

MIRA GRANT

—

Professor Michael Mason is the current head of our Biology Department. Prior to joining the staff here at Berkeley, he was at the University of Redmond for six years. His lovely wife, Stacy, is a horticulture fan, and his son, Phillip, is a fan of cartoons and of chasing pigeons...

June 12, 2014:
The lower stratosphere.

Freed from its secure lab environment, Alpha-RC007 floated serene and unaware on the air currents of the stratosphere. It did not enjoy freedom; it did not abhor freedom; it did not feel anything, not even the cool breezes holding it aloft. In the absence of a living host, the hybrid virus was inert, waiting for something to come along and shock it into a semblance of life.

On the ground, far away, Dr. Alexander Kellis was weeping without shame over the destruction of his lab, and making dire predictions about what could happen now that his creation was loose in the world. Like Dr. Frankenstein before him, he had created with only the best of intentions and now found himself facing an uncertain future. His lover tried to soothe him and was rebuffed by a grief too vast and raw to be put into words.

Alpha-RC007—colloquially known as "the Kellis cure"—did not grieve, or love, or worry about the future. Alpha-RC007 only drifted.

The capsid structure of Alpha-RC007 was superficially identical to the structure of the common rhinovirus, being composed of viral proteins locking together to form an icosahedron. The binding proteins, however, were more closely related to the coronavirus ancestors of the hybrid, creating a series of keys against which no natural immune system could lock itself. The five viral proteins forming the capsid structure were equally mismatched: two from one family, two from the other, and the fifth...

The fifth was purely a credit to the man who constructed it, and had nothing of Nature's handiwork in its construction. It was a tiny protein, smaller even than the diminutive VP4 which made the rhinovirus so infectious, and formed a ring of Velcro-like hooks around the outside of the icosahedron. That little hook was the key to Alpha-RC007's universal infection rate. By latching on and refusing to be dislodged, the virus could take as much time as it needed to find a way to properly colonize its host. Once inside, the other specially tailored traits would have their opportunity to shine. All the man-made protein had to do was buy the time to make it past the walls.

The wind currents eddied around the tiny viral particles, allowing them to drop somewhat lower in the stratosphere. Here, a flock of geese was taking advantage of

Countdown

the air currents at the very edge of the atmospheric layer, their honks sounding through the thin air like car alarms. One, banking to adjust her course, raised a wing just a few inches higher, tilting herself hard to the right and letting her feathers brush through the upper currents.

As her feathers swept through the air, they collected dust and pollen—and a few opportunistically drifting particles of Alpha-RC007. The hooks on the outside of the virus promptly latched onto the goose's wing, not aware, only reacting to the change in their environment. This was not a suitable host, and so the bulk of the virus remained inert, waiting, letting itself be carried along by its unwitting escort back down to the planet's surface.

Honking loudly, the geese flew on. In the air currents above them, the rest of the viral particles freed from Dr. Alexander Kellis's lab drifted, waiting for their own escorts to come along, scoop them up, and allow them to freely roam the waiting Earth. There is nothing so patient, in this world or any other, as a virus searching for a host.

—

We're looking at clear skies here in the Midwest, with temperatures spiking to a new high for this summer—so grab your sunscreen and plan to spend another lazy weekend staying out of the sun! Pollen counts are projected to be low...

June 13, 2014: Denver, Colorado.

Suzanne Amberlee had been waiting to box up her daughter's room almost since the day Amanda was first diagnosed with leukemia. Her therapist said it was a "coping mechanism" for her, and that it was completely healthy for her to spend hours thinking about boxes and storage and what to do with things too precious to be given to Goodwill. As the parent of a sick child, she'd been all too willing to believe that, grasping at any comfort that her frightened mind could offer her. She had made her lists long ago. These were the things she would keep; these were the things she would send to family members; these were the things she would give to Amanda's friends. Simple lines, drawn in ink on the ledger of her heart.

That was thought. The reality of standing in her little girl's bedroom and imagining it empty, stripped of all the things that made it Amanda's, was almost more than she could bear. After weeks of struggling with herself, she had finally been able to close her hand on the doorknob and open the bedroom door. She still wasn't able to force herself across the threshold.

This room contained all Amanda's things—all the things she'd ever have the opportunity to own. The stuffed toys she had steadfastly refused to admit to outgrowing, saying they had been her only friends when she was sick and she wouldn't abandon them now. Her bookshelves, cluttered with knick-knacks and soccer trophies as much as books. Her framed poster showing the structure of Marburg EX19, given to her by Dr. Wells after the first clinical trials began showing positive results. Suzanne could picture that day when she closed her eyes. Amanda, looking so weak and pale, and Dr. Wells, their savior, smiling like the sun.

"This little fellow is your best friend now, Amanda," that was what he'd said on that beautiful afternoon where having a future suddenly seemed possible again. "Take good care of it and it will take good care of you."

Rage swept over Suzanne in a sudden hot wave. She opened her eyes, glaring across the room at the photographic disease. Where was it when her little girl was dying? Marburg EX19 was supposed to save her baby's life, and in the end, it had let her down; it had let Amanda die. What was the good of all this—the pain, the endless hours spent in hospital beds, the promises they never got to keep—if the damn disease couldn't save Amanda's life?

Countdown

Never mind that Amanda died in a car crash. Never mind that cancer had nothing to do with it. Marburg EX19 was supposed to save her, and it had failed.

"I hate you," Suzanne whispered, and turned away. She couldn't deal with the bedroom; not today, maybe not ever. Maybe she would just sell the house, leave Amanda's things where they were, and let them be dealt with by the new owners. They could filter through the spindrift of Amanda's life without seeing her face, without hearing her voice talking about college plans and careers. They could put things in boxes without breaking their hearts.

If there was anything more terrible for a parent than burying a child, Suzanne Amberlee couldn't imagine what it would be. Her internal battle over for another day—over, and lost—she turned away, heading down the stairs. Maybe tomorrow she could empty out that room. Maybe tomorrow, she could start boxing things away. Maybe tomorrow, she could start the process of letting Amanda go.

Maybe tomorrow. But probably not.

Suzanne Amberlee walked away, unaware of the small viral colony living in her own body, nested deep in the tissue of her lungs. Content in its accidental home, Marburg EX19 slept, waiting for the trigger that would startle it into wakefulness. It was patient; it had all the time in the world.

—

39

MIRA GRANT

> *Amanda Amberlee is survived by her mother, Suzanne Amberlee. In lieu of flowers, the family asks that donations be sent to the Colorado Cancer Research Center...*

June 15, 2014: Reston, Virginia.

Alex?"

The lights were off in the main lab, leaving it in claustrophobic darkness. Most of the staff had long since gone home for the night. That made sense; it had been past eleven when John Kellis pulled into the parking lot, and the only car parked in front of the building was his husband's familiar bottle-green Ford. He hadn't bothered to call before coming over. Maybe some men strayed to bars or strip clubs. Not Alex. When Alex went running to his other lover, he was always running to the lab.

John paused before pushing open the door leading into the inner office. The last thing he wanted to do was upset Alex further when he was already so delicate. "Sweetheart? Are you in here?"

There was still no answer. John's heart started beating a little faster, spurred on by fear. The pressure had been immense since the break-in. Years of research gone; millions of dollars in private funding lost; and perhaps worst of all, Alex's sense of certainty that the world would somehow start playing fair, shattered. John wasn't sure that he could recover from that, and if Alex couldn't recover, then John didn't think he could recover, either.

This lab had been their life for so long. Vacations had been planned around ongoing research; even the question of whether or not to have a baby had been put off, again and again, by the demands of Alex's work. They had both believed it was worth it for so long. Was one act of eco-terrorism going to change all that?

John was suddenly very afraid that it was.

"I'm back here, John," said Alex's voice. It was soft, dull…dead. Heart still hammering, John turned his walk into a half-jog, rounding the corner to find himself looking at the glass window onto the former hot room. Alex was standing in front of it, just like he had so many times before, but his shoulders were stooped. He looked defeated.

"Alex, you have to stop doing this to yourself." John's heartbeat slowed as he saw that his husband was unharmed. He walked the rest of the distance between them, stopping behind Alex and sliding his arms around the other man's shoulders. "Come on. Come home with me."

"I can't." Alex indicated the window. "Look."

The hot room had been re-sealed after the break-in; maybe they couldn't stop their home-brewed pathogens from getting out, but they could stop anything new from getting in. The rhesus monkeys and guinea pigs were back in their cages. Some were eating, some were sleeping; others were just going about their business, oblivious to the humans watching over them.

"I don't understand." John squinted, frowning at the glass. "What am I supposed to be seeing? They all look perfectly normal."

"I've bathed them in every cold sample I could find, along with half a dozen flus and an airborne form of syphilis. One of the guinea pigs died, but the necropsy didn't show any sign that it was either an infection or the cure that killed it. Sometimes guinea pigs just die."

"I'm sorry. I don't understand the problem. What's wrong with your lab animals being healthy?"

Alexander Kellis pulled away from his husband, expression anguished as he turned to face him. "I can't tell which ones have caught the cure and which haven't. It's undetectable in a living subject. After the break-in, we're probably infected, too. And *I don't know what it will do in a human host*. We weren't ready." He started to cry, looking very young and very old at the same time. "I may have just killed us all."

"Oh, honey, no." John gathered him close, making soothing noises...but his eyes were on the animals behind the glass. The perfectly healthy, perfectly normal animals. Suddenly, it seemed like he couldn't look away.

—

MIRA GRANT

Dr. Alexander Kellis has thus far refused to comment on the potential risks posed by his untested "cure for the common cold," released three days ago by a group calling itself "the Mayday Army"...

June 18, 2014: Atlanta, Georgia.

The best description for the atmosphere at the Centers for Disease Control in Atlanta, Georgia, was "tense." Everyone was waiting for the other shoe to drop, and had been waiting since reports first came in describing the so-called "Mayday Army's" release of an experimental pathogen into the atmosphere. The tension only intensified when Dr. Alexander Kellis responded to requests for more information on the pathogen by supplying his research, which detailed, at length, the infectious nature of his hybridized creation.

One of the administrative assistants had probably put it best when she looked at the projected infection maps in horror and said, "If he'd been working with rabies or something, he would have just killed us all."

If he was being completely honest with himself, Dr. Ian Matras wasn't entirely sure that Alexander Kellis *hadn't* just killed them all, entirely without intending to, entirely with the best of intentions. The proteins composing the capsid shell on Alpha-RC007 were ingeniously engineered, something that had been a good thing—increased stability, increased predictability in behavior—right up until the moment when the idiots in the Mayday Army broke the seals keeping the world and the virus apart. Now those same proteins made Alpha-RC007 extremely virulent, extremely contagious, and, worst of all, extremely difficult to detect in a living host. The lab animals they'd requested from Dr. Kellis's lab in Reston were known to be infected, but showed almost no signs of illness; four out of five blood tests would come up negative for the presence of Alpha-RC007, only to have the fifth show a thriving infection. Alpha-RC007 *hid*. It could be spurred to reveal itself by introducing another infection into the host...and that was when Alpha-RC007 became truly terrifying.

Alpha-RC007 was engineered to cure the common cold, something it accomplished by setting itself up as a competing, and superior, infection. Once it was in the body, it simply never went away. The specific structure of its capsid shell somehow tricked the human immune system into believing that Alpha-RC007 was another form of helper cell—and, in a way, it was. Alpha-RC007 wanted to help. Watching it attack and envelop other viruses that entered the body was a chilling demonstration of perfect biological efficiency. Alpha-RC007 saw; Alpha-RC007 killed. Alpha-RC007 tolerated no other infections in the body.

Countdown

What was going to happen the first time Alpha-RC007 decided the human immune system counted as an infection? No one knew, and the virus had thus far resisted any and all attempts to remove it from a living host. Unless a treatment could be found before Kellis's creation decided to become hostile, Dr. Matras was very afraid that the entire world was going to learn just how vicious Alpha-RC007 could be.

He sat at his desk, watching the infection models as they spread out across North America and the world, and wondered how long they really had before they found out whether or not the Mayday Army had managed to destroy mankind—with the help of Dr. Alexander Kellis, of course.

"Cheer up, Ian!" called one of his colleagues, passing by on the way to the break room. "A pandemic disease that makes you healthy isn't exactly the worst thing we've ever had to deal with."

"And what's it going to do to us in a year, Chris?" Dr. Matras shot back.

Dr. Chris Sinclair grinned. "Raise the dead, of course," he said. "Don't you ever go to the movies?" Then he walked away, leaving Dr. Matras alone to brood.

—

The Centers for Disease Control have issued a statement asking that people remain calm in the wake of the release of an unidentified pathogen from the Virginia-based lab of

Dr. Alexander Kellis. "We do not, as yet, have any indication that this disease is harmful to humans," said Dr. Chris Sinclair. A seven-year veteran of the Epidemic Intelligence Service, Dr. Sinclair graduated from Princeton...

July 2, 2014: Denver, Colorado.

Janice Barton knocked twice on the door to Dr. Wells's office before opening it and stepping inside, expression drawn. "Do you think you can see three more patients today?" she asked, without preamble.

"What?" Dr. Wells looked up from his paperwork, fingers clenching involuntarily on his pen. "I've already seen nine patients since four! I've barely finished filing the insurance information for Mrs. Bridge. How am I supposed to see three more before we close?"

"Because if you'll agree to see three more, I can probably convince the other nineteen to come back tomorrow," Janice replied. For the first time, Dr. Wells realized how harried his normally composed administrative assistant looked. Her nails were chipped. Somehow, that seemed like the biggest danger sign of all. A man-made virus was on the loose, Marburg Amberlee was doing… something…and Janice had allowed her manicure to fray.

"I'll see the three most in need of attention, and then I have to close for the night," he said, putting down his pen as he stood. "If I don't get some sleep, I won't be of any use to anyone."

"They're all in need of attention. I can't choose. But thank you," said Janice, and withdrew.

She was gone by the time he emerged from his office, retreating to wherever it was she went when she was tired of dealing with the madhouse of the waiting room. On the days when it *was* a madhouse, anyway. This was definitely one of those days. The gathered patients set up a clamor as soon as he appeared, all of them waving for his attention, some of them even shouting. Dr. Wells stopped, looking at the crowd, and wondered if the other doctors involved in the Marburg Amberlee tests were having the same experience.

He was deeply afraid that they were.

The trouble wasn't the patients themselves; they looked as hale and healthy as ever, which explained how they were able to yell quite so loudly for his attention. Their cancers were gone, or under control, constantly besieged by their defensive Marburg Amberlee infections. It was the people they had brought to the office with them that presented the truly alarming problem. Husbands and wives, parents and children, they sat next to their previously ill relatives with glazed eyes, taking shallow, pained-sounding breaths. Some of them were bleeding from the nose or tear ducts—just a trickle, nothing life-threatening, but that little trickle was

enough to terrify Dr. Wells, making his bowels feel loose and his stomach crawl.

They were manifesting the early signs of a Marburg Amberlee infection, during the brief phase where the body's immune system attempted to treat the helper virus as an invasion. That was the one stage of infection that could be truly harmful; when Marburg Amberlee was hit, it hit back, and it was more interested in defeating the opposition than it was in preserving the host. These people were infected, all of them.

And that simply wasn't possible. Marburg Amberlee wasn't transmissible through casual contact—or at least, it wasn't supposed to be, and if the trials had been wrong about that, what else could they have been wrong about? Pointing almost at random, he said, "You, you, and you. I can see you before we close. Everyone else, I'm very sorry, but you're going to have to come back tomorrow. See Janice before you leave, she'll set you up with an appointment."

Groans and shouts of protest spread through the room. "My baby's sick!" shouted one woman. A year before, she'd been dying of lung cancer. She'd called him a miracle worker. Now she was glaring at him like he was the devil incarnate. "What are you going to do about it?"

"I'm going to see you tomorrow," said Dr. Wells firmly, and waved for the chosen three to step through the door between the reception area and the examination rooms. He retreated with relief, the feeling of dread growing stronger.

He honestly had no idea what he was going to do.

Countdown

—

Rumors of an outbreak of hemorrhagic fever in and around the Colorado Cancer Research Center have as yet been unsubstantiated. The center's head doctor, Daniel Wells, is unavailable for comment at this time.

July 4, 2014:
Allentown, Pennsylvania.

The streets of Allentown were decked in patriotic red, white, and blue, symbolizing freedom from oppression—symbolizing independence. That word had never seemed so relevant. Brandon Majors walked along, smiling at every red streamer and blue rosette, wishing he could jump up on a bench and tell everyone in earshot how *he* was responsible for their *true* independence. How *he* working in the best interests of mankind, had granted them independence from illness, freedom from the flu, and the liberty to use their sick days sitting on the beach, sipping soft drinks and enjoying their liberty from The Man! They'd probably give him a medal, or at least carry him around the city on their shoulders.

Sadly, their triumphant march would probably be interrupted by the local police. The Man had his dogs looking for the brave members of the Mayday Army, calling them "eco-terrorists" and making dire statements about how they'd endangered the public health. Endangered it how? By setting the people free from the tyranny of Big Pharma? If that was endangerment, then maybe it was time for *everything* to be endangered. Even The Man would have to admit that, once he saw how much better the world was thanks to Brandon and his brave compatriots.

Brandon walked toward home, lost in thoughts of glories to come once the Mayday Army could come out of the shadows and announce themselves to the world as saviors of the common man. What was the statute of limitations on eco-terrorism, anyway? Would it be reduced—at least in their case—once people started realizing what a gift they had been given? Maybe—

He turned the corner, and saw the police cars surrounding the house. Brandon stopped dead, watching wide-eyed as men in uniform carried a kicking, weeping Hazel down the front porch steps and toward a black and white police van. The back doors opened as they approached, and three more officers reached out to pull Hazel inside. He could hear her sobbing, protesting, demanding to know what they thought she'd done wrong.

There was nothing he could do.

He repeated that to himself over and over again as he took two steps backward, turned, and began to run. The Man had found them out. Somehow, impossibly, The Man had found them out, and now Hazel was going to be a martyr to the cause. There was nothing he could do. The pigs already had her. They were already taking her away, and this wasn't some big Hollywood block-buster action movie; he couldn't charge in there and somehow rescue her right out from under their noses. Her parents had money. They would find a way to buy her freedom. In the meantime, there was nothing, nothing, *nothing* he could do. Hazel wouldn't want him to give himself up for her. He was absolutely certain of that. One of them had to get away. One of them had to escape The Man.

Brandon was still repeating that to himself when the sirens started behind him, and the bullhorn-distorted voice blared forth, saying, "Mr. Majors, please stop running, or we will be forced to shoot." The owner of the voice didn't sound like she'd particularly mind.

Brandon stopped. Without turning, he raised his hands in the air, and shouted, "I am an American citizen! I am being unfairly detained!" His voice quaked on the last word, somewhat ruining the brave revolutionary image he was trying to project.

Heavy footsteps on the street behind him announced the approach of the cop seconds before Brandon's hands were grabbed and wrenched behind his back. "You call this unfair detention? You should feel lucky we're arresting you at all, and not just publishing your name and address in the paper, you idiot," hissed the officer, her voice harsh and close to his ear. "You think this country loves terrorists?"

"We were doing it for you!" he wailed.

"Tell it to the judge," she said, and turned him forcefully around before leading him away.

—

The ringleaders of the so-called "Mayday Army" were arrested today following a tip from one of their former followers. His name has not been released at this time. Brandon Majors, 25, and Hazel Allen, 23, are residents of Allentown, Pennsylvania. Drug paraphernalia was recovered at the scene...

July 4, 2014: Berkeley, California.

The Berkeley Marina was packed with parents, children, college students on summer break, dog walkers, senior citizens, and members of every other social group in the Bay Area. A Great Dane ran by, towing his bikini-clad owner on a pair of roller skates. A group of teens walked in the opposite direction, dressed in such bright colors that they resembled a flock of exotic birds. They were chattering in the rapid-fire patois specific to their generation, that transitory form of language developed by every group of teens since language began. Stacy Mason paused in watching her husband chase her son around the dock to watch the group go past, their laughter bright as bells in the summer afternoon.

She'd been one of those girls, once, all sunshine and serenity, absolutely confident that the world would give her whatever she asked it for. Wouldn't they be surprised when they realized that sometimes, what you asked for wasn't really what you wanted?

"Where are you right now?" Michael stepped up behind her, slipping his arms around her waist and planting a kiss against the side of her neck. "It's a beautiful summer day here in sunny Berkeley, California, and the laser show will be starting soon. You might want to come back."

"Just watching the crowd." Stacy twisted around to face her husband, smiling up at him with amusement. "Aren't *you* supposed to be watching something? Namely, our son?"

"I have been discarded in favor of a more desirable babysitter," said Michael gravely. His tone was solemn, but his eyes were amused.

"Oh? And who would that be?"

Behind her, Phillip shouted jubilantly, "*Oggie!*"

"Ahhhh. I see." Stacy turned to see Phillip chasing Maize in an unsteady circle while Marigold sat nearby, calmly watching the action. Mr. Connors was holding Marigold's leash; Maize's leash was being allowed to drag on the ground behind him while the Golden Retriever fled playfully from his playmate. "Hello, Mr. Connors! Where's Marla?"

"Hello, Stacy!" Mr. Connors turned to wave, one eye still on the fast-moving pair. "She went down the dock to get us some lemonades. Hope you don't mind my absconding with your boy."

"Not at all. It'll do both of us some good if our respective charges can run off a little of their excess energy."

Countdown

Stacy leaned up against Michael, watching as Maize and Phillip chased each other, one laughing, the other with tail wagging madly. "Maybe they can wear each other out."

Michael snorted. "That'll be the day. I think that boy is powered by plutonium."

"And whose fault would that be, hmm? I just *had* to go and marry a scientist. I could have held out for a rock star, but no, I wanted the glamour and romance of being a professor's wife."

This time, Michael laughed out loud. "Believe me, I count my blessings every day when I remember that you could have held out for a rock star."

Stacy smiled at him warmly before looking around at the crowd, the sky, the water. Phillip was laughing, his sound blending with the cries of seagulls and the barking of over-excited dogs to form just one more part of the great noise that was the voice of humanity. She had never heard anything so beautiful in her life.

"I think we should all be counting our blessings every day," she said finally. "Life doesn't get any better than this."

"Life can always get better." Michael kissed her one more time, his lips lingering lightly against her cheek. "Just you wait and see. This time next year, we won't be able to imagine looking back on this summer without thinking 'Oh, you had no idea; just you wait and see.'"

"I hope you're right," said Stacy, and kissed him back.

—

The annual Fourth of July laser show at the Berkeley Marina was a huge success this year, drawing record crowds. The laser show, which replaced the traditional firework displays as of 2012, has become a showpiece of the year's calendar, and this year was no different. With designs programmed by the UC Berkeley Computer Science Department...

July 7, 2014: Manhattan, New York.

In the month since his report on the so-called "Kellis cure" had first appeared, Robert Stalnaker had received a level of attention and adulation—and yes, vitriol and hatred—that he had previously only dreamed of. His inbox was packed every morning with people both applauding and condemning his decision to reveal Dr. Alexander Kellis's scientific violation of the American public. Was *he* the one who told the Mayday Army to break into Kellis's lab, doing thousands of dollars of damage and unleashing millions of dollars of research into the open air? No, he was not. He was simply a concerned member of the American free press, doing his job and reporting the news.

The fact that he had essentially fabricated the story had stopped bothering him after the third interview request he received. By the Monday following the Fourth of July, he would have been honestly shocked if someone had asked him about the truth behind his lies. As far as he was concerned, he'd been telling the truth. Maybe it wasn't the truth that Dr. Kellis had intended, but it was the one he'd created. All Stalnaker did was report it to the world.

Best of all, he hadn't seen anyone sneezing or coughing in almost two weeks. Whatever craziness Kellis had been cooking up in that lab of his, it did what it was supposed to do. Throw out the Kleenex and cancel that order for chicken soup, can I hear an amen from the congregation?

"Amen," murmured Stalnaker, pushing open the door to his paper's New York office. A cool blast of climate-controlled air flowed out into the hall, chasing away the stickiness of the New York summer. He stepped into the room, letting the door swing shut behind him, and waited for the applause that inevitably followed his arrival. He was, after all, the one who had single-handedly increased circulation almost fifteen percent in under a week.

The applause didn't come. Instead, an uneasy silence fell as people stopped their work and turned to stare. Bemused, he looked around the room and saw his editor bearing down on him with a grim expression on his face and a toothpick bouncing between his lips as he frantically chewed it into splinters. The toothpicks had been intended as an aid when he'd quit smoking the year before. Somehow, they'd just never gone away.

"Stalnaker!" he growled, shoving the toothpick off to one side of his mouth as he demanded, "Where the hell have you been? Don't you check your email?"

Countdown

"Not during breakfast," said Stalnaker, taken aback by his editor's tone. Don never talked to him like that. Harshly, sure, and sometimes coldly, but never like he'd done something too wrong to be articulated; never like he was a puppy who'd made a mess on the carpet. "Why? Did I miss a political scandal or something while I was having a bagel?"

Don Nutick paused, forcing himself to take a deep, slow breath before he said, "No. You missed the Pennsylvania police department announcing that the ringleaders of the Mayday Army were taken into custody Friday afternoon."

"What?" Stalnaker stared at him, suddenly fully alert. "You're telling me they actually *caught* the guys? How the hell did they manage that?"

"One of their own decided to rat them out. Said that it wasn't right for them to get away with what they'd done." Don shook his head. "They're not releasing the guy's name yet. Still, whoever managed to get an exclusive interview with him, why I bet that person could write his or her own ticket. Maybe even convince a sympathetic editor not to fire his ass over faking a report that's getting the paper threatened with a lawsuit."

"Lawsuit?"

"I told you you needed to check your email more."

Stalnaker scoffed. "They'll never get it to stick."

"You sure of that?"

There was a moment of silence before Stalnaker said, reluctantly, "I guess I'm going to Pennsylvania."

"Yes," Don agreed. "I guess you are."

—

While the identity of the Mayday Army's deserter has been protected thus far, it must be asked: why did this man decide to turn on his compatriots? What did he see in that lab that caused him to change his ways? We don't know, but we're going to find out...

July 7, 2014:
Somewhere in North America.

The location doesn't matter: what happened, when it happened, happened all over North America at the same time. There was no single index case. It all began, and ended, too fast for that sort of record-keeping to endure.

On migratory bird and weather balloon, on drifting debris and anchored in tiny gusts of wind, Alpha-RC007 made its way down from the stratosphere to the world below. When it encountered a suitable mammalian host, it latched on with its tiny man-made protein hooks, holding itself in place while it found a way to invade, colonize, and spread. The newborn infections were invisible to the naked eye, and their only symptom was a total lack of symptoms. Their hosts enjoyed a level of health that was remarkable mostly because none of them noticed, or realized how lucky they were. It was a viral golden age.

It lasted less than a month. Say July 7th, for lack of a precise date; say Columbus, Ohio, for lack of a precise location. July 7th, 2014, Columbus: the end of the world begins.

The only carrier of Marburg Amberlee in Columbus was Lauren Morris, a thirty-eight year old woman celebrating her second lease on life by taking a road trip across the United States. She had begun her Marburg Amberlee treatments almost exactly a year before, and had seen a terminal diagnosis dwindle into nothing. If you'd asked her, she would have called it a miracle of science. She would have been correct.

Lauren's first encounter with Alpha-RC007 occurred at an open-air farmer's market. She picked up a jar of homemade jam, examining the label with a curious eye before deciding, finally, not to make the purchase. The jam remained behind, but the virus that had collected on her fingers did not. It clung, waiting for an opportunity—an opportunity it got less than five minutes later, when Lauren wiped a piece of dust away from her eye. Alpha-RC007 transferred from her fingers to the vulnerable mucus membrane inside her eyelid, and from there made its entrance to the body.

The initial stages of the Alpha-RC007 infection followed the now-familiar pattern, invading the body's cells like a common virus, only to slip quietly out again, leaving copies of itself behind. The only cells to be

Countdown

actually destroyed in the process were the other infections Alpha-RC007 encountered in the host body. These were turned into tiny virus-factories, farming on a microscopic scale. Several minor ailments Lauren was not even aware of were found brewing in her body, and summarily destroyed in Alpha-RC007's quest for sole dominion.

Then, deep in the tissue of Lauren's lungs, Alpha-RC007 encountered something new; something which was confusing to the virus, in as much as anything can ever confuse a virus. This strange new thing had a structure as alien to the world as Alpha-RC007's own: half-natural, half-reconfigured and transformed to suit a new purpose.

Behaving according to the protocols that were the whole of its existence, Alpha-RC007 approached the stranger, using its delicate protein hooks to attempt infiltration. The stranger responded in kind, their protein hooks tangling together until they were like so much viral thread, too intertwined to tell where one ended and the next began. This happened a thousand times in the body of Lauren Morris. Many of those joinings ended with the destruction of one or both viral bodies, their structures unable to correctly lock together.

The rest found an unexpected kinship in the locks and controls their human creators had installed, and began, without releasing one another, to exchange genetic material in a beautiful dance that had begun when life on this world was born, and would last until that life was completely gone. Oblivious to the second miracle of

69

science that was now happening inside her, Lauren Morris went about her day. She had never been a mother before. Before the sun went down, she would be one of the many mothers to give birth to Kellis-Amberlee.

—

It's a beautiful summer here in Ohio, and we have a great many events planned for these sweet summer nights. Visit the downtown Columbus Farmer's Market, where you can sample new delights from our local farms. Who knows what you might discover? Meanwhile, the summer concert series kicks off...

July 8, 2014: Atlanta, Georgia.

Chris Sinclair's time at the CDC had been characterized by an almost pathological degree of calm. He remained completely relaxed even during outbreaks of unknown origin, calling on his EIS training and his natural tendency to "not sweat the small stuff" in order to keep his head while everyone around him was losing theirs. When asked, he attributed his attitude to growing up in Santa Cruz, California, where the local surf culture taught everyone to chill out already.

Chris Sinclair wasn't chilling out anymore. Chris Sinclair was terrified.

They still had no reliable test for the Kellis cure. Instead of charting the path of the infection, they were falling back on an old EIS trick and charting the absence of infection. Any place where the normal chain of summer colds and flu had been broken, they marked on the maps as a possible outbreak of the Kellis cure. It wasn't a sure-fire method of detection—sometimes people were just healthy, without any genetically engineered virus to explain the reasons why. Still. If only half the people showing up as potential Kellis cure infections were sick...

If only half the people showing up as potential Kellis cure infections were sick with this sickness that wasn't a sickness at all, then that meant that this stuff was spreading like wildfire and there was no way they could stop it. If they put out a health advisory recommending people avoid close contact with anyone who looked excessively healthy, they'd have "cure parties" springing up nationwide. It was the only possible result. Before the chicken pox vaccine was commonly available, parents used to have chicken pox parties, choosing sickness now to guarantee health later. They'd do it again. And then, if the Kellis cure had a second stage—something that would have shown up in the human trials Alexander Kellis never had the opportunity to conduct—they would be in for a world of trouble.

Assuming, of course, that they weren't already.

"Still think we shouldn't be too worried about a pandemic that just makes everybody well?"

"Ian." Chris raised his head, giving a half-ashamed shrug as he said, "I didn't hear you come in."

"You were pretty engrossed in those papers. Are those the updated maps of the projected spread?"

"They are." Chris chuckled mirthlessly. "You'll be happy to know that our last North American holdouts have succumbed to the mysterious good health that's been going around. We have infection patterns in Newfoundland and Alaska. In both cases, I was able to find records showing that the pattern manifested shortly after someone from another of the suspected infection zones came to town. It's spreading. If it's not already everywhere in the world, it will be soon."

"Have there been any reported symptoms? Anything that might point to a mutation?" Ian Matras filled his mug from the half-full pot sitting on the department hot plate, grimacing at the taste even as he kept on drinking. It was bitter but strong. That was what he needed to get through this catastrophe.

"I was wondering when you'd get to asking about the bad part."

"There was a good part?"

Chris ignored him, shuffling through the papers on his desk until he found a red folder. Flipping it open, he read, "Sudden increased salivation in the trial subjects for the McKenzie-Beatts TB treatment. That was the one using genetically modified yellow fever? Three deaths in a modified malaria test group. We're still waiting for the last body to arrive, but in the two we have, it looks like their man-made malaria suddenly started attacking their red blood cells. Wiped them out faster than their bone marrow could rebuild them."

"The Kellis cure doesn't play nicely with the other children," observed Ian.

"No, it doesn't." Chris looked up, expression grim. "The rest of these are dealing with subjects from the

Colorado cancer trials. The ones that used the live version of the modified Marburg virus. They're expressing the same symptoms as everyone else…but their families are starting to show signs of the Marburg variant. Somehow, interaction with the Kellis cure is teaching it how to *spread*. That, or it was already spreading on a sub-clinical level, and now the Kellis cure is waking it up."

Ian stared at him, coffee forgotten. "Oh, Jesus."

"I'm pretty sure he's not listening, but you can call him if it makes you feel better," said Chris. He handed his colleague the folder and the two of them turned back to their work. They were trying to prevent the inevitable. They both knew that. But that didn't mean they didn't have to try.

—

Effective immediately, all human clinical trials utilizing live strains of any genetically modified virus have been suspended. All records and patient lists for these trials must be submitted to the CDC office in Atlanta, Georgia, by noon EST on July 10th. Failure to comply may result in federal charges…

July 10, 2014: Reston, Virginia.

The sound of the front door slamming brought Alexander Kellis out of his light doze. He'd managed to drift off on the couch while he was waiting for John to come home with dinner—the first time he'd slept in days. His first feeling, once the disorientation passed, was irritation. Couldn't John be a little more careful? Didn't he know how exhausted he was?

Then he realized that he wasn't hearing any footsteps. Annoyance faded into concern. "John?" Alex stood, nudging his glasses back into place as he started, warily, toward the foyer.

Jonathan and Alexander Kellis lived in a sprawling house that was really too big for just the two of them, something they'd been intending to fix once Alex's research paid off and early retirement became a viable option. Neither of them really wanted to have children without knowing that one parent, at the very

least, would be able to be home for the first few years—
and whether they adopted or found a surrogate, they'd
always known that one day, they'd fill that empty house
with children.

At the moment, however, all that filled the house
was silence. And the silence was somehow terrifying.
"John?" he repeated, and stepped into the darkened
foyer, fumbling for the light switch with one hand. He
found it and clicked it on, illuminating the room...and
then he froze, eyes going very wide, mouth going very
dry as he tried to process what he was seeing.

How John had managed to make it into the house
under his own power was a mystery that might never be
solved. Into the house, and no further. He was collapsed
across the hardwood floor, limp and boneless. A smear
of blood on the wall showed where he had tried to grab
hold as he was falling.

"*John!*" Alex broke out of his fugue, closing the distance between them in three long steps. He barely even
felt the pain when his knees slammed into the ground.
Fumbling for a pulse with one hand, he said, "John?
Sweetheart? Can you hear me?"

John moaned. It was a soft, hollow sound, like the
kind made by ghosts in bad horror movies, and it made
Alex's blood run cold. "Alex?"

"I'm here, honey. Be still. I'm going to call 911. You
just...you just keep still."

"They beat me, Alex." John Kellis managed, somehow, to roll over enough to look up at the man he'd

76

loved since college, when they were both so damn
young, and so wonderfully full of optimistic fantasies.
"Line at the Chinese place was too long. I went for
Indian. Drove past the lab...lights were on. I thought
you'd gone out again. I thought you were choosing
those *damn* monkeys over me." The venom in his voice
made Alex jump. Oblivious, John continued, "Stopped
the car. Went in to get you...found them. They let
them out, Alex. They let them all out." John closed his
eyes. "I'm sorry. I couldn't stop them."

"Stop who?" asked Alex, frozen.

"Said you were...experimenting on animals. Said it
was unethical. They said...we deserved what we got." John
sighed. "They said we deserved...everything we got."

"Stay with me, sweetheart. Stay awake. Stay with
me." Alex fumbled his cell phone out of his pocket,
dialing as he raised it to his ear. "Hello, 911? This is
Alexander Kellis. My husband has been badly beaten.
We're located at..." He took John's hand in his as he
gave the address, and held it until the ambulance arrived,
waiting for John to say something—anything—to let
him know that it would be all right. To let him know
that this wasn't how it ended.

John didn't say a word. The ambulance arrived, and
the EMTs loaded John into the back, leaving Alex to
follow in his car. If John woke up on the way to the hospital, no one noticed; no one heard whatever he might
have said. Jonathan Kellis was pronounced dead on
arrival at 9:53 PM on July 10th, 2014. If there was any

Countdown

mercy in this—and there was no mercy to be seen, not then—it was that he died early enough to stay that way.

—

Jonathan Kellis, husband of infamous genetic engineer Dr. Alexander Kellis, died last night following a beating at the hands of unidentified assailants. Mr. Kellis had apparently surprised them in the act of vandalizing Dr. Kellis's lab. No suspects have been identified at this time...

July 13, 2014:
Allentown, Pennsylvania.

After six days of snooping, bribery, and the occasional outright lie, Robert Stalnaker had finally achieved his goal: a meeting with the college student who had blown the whistle on the leaders of the Mayday Army. It had been more difficult than he'd expected. Since the death of Dr. Kellis's husband—something which was *not* his fault; not only did his article not say "break into the lab and free the experimental virus," it certainly never said "beat the man's lover to a bloody pulp if you get the chance"—the security had closed in tighter around the man who was regarded as the state's star, and really only, witness to the actions of the Mayday Army. Robert carefully got out his pocket recorder, checking to be sure the memory buffer was clear. He was only going to get one shot at this.

The door opened, and a skinny, anxious-looking college boy stepped into the room, followed by a pair of visibly armed police officers. Stalnaker would have attempted to convince them to leave, but frankly, after what had happened to John Kellis...these were unsettled times. Having a few authority figures present might be good for everyone involved. Especially since they were authority figures with guns.

"Thank you for meeting with me, Matthew," he said, standing and extending his hand to be shaken. The college boy had a light grip, like he was afraid of breaking something. Stalnaker made a note of that, even as he kept on smiling. "I'm Robert Stalnaker, with *The Clarion News* in New York. I really do appreciate it."

"You're the one who wrote that article," said Matt, pulling his hand away and sitting down on the other side of the table. His eyes darted from side to side like a cornered dog's, assessing the exit routes. "They would never have done it if you hadn't done that first."

"Done what, exactly?" Stalnaker produced a notepad and pencil from his pocket, making sure Matt saw him getting ready to take notes. The recorder was already running, but somehow, it never caused the Pavlovian need to speak that he could trigger with a carefully poised pencil. "I just want to know your side of the story, son."

Matt took a shaky breath. "Look. I didn't—nobody told me this was going to be a whole thing, you know? This girl I know just told me that Brandon and Hazel could

Countdown

hook me up with some good weed. I was coming off of finals, I was tense, I needed to relax a little. That was all."

"I understand," said Stalnaker encouragingly. "When I was in college, I heard the siren song of good weed more than a few times. Was the weed good?"

"Aw, man, it was *awesome.*" Matt's eyes lit up. Only for a moment; the light quickly dimmed, and he continued more cautiously, "Anyway, everybody started talking about revolution, and sticking it to The Man, and how this dude Kellis was going to screw us all by only giving his cold-cure to the people who could afford it. I should have done the research, you know? I should have looked it up. It's *contagious*, see? Even if we'd left it alone, let Dr. Kellis finish his testing, we would have all been able to get it in the end. If it worked."

Something about the haunted tone in Matt's voice made Stalnaker sit up a little bit straighter. "Do you think it doesn't work? Can you support that?"

"Oh, it works. Nobody's had a cold in weeks. We're the killers of the common cold. Hi-ho, give somebody a medal." Matt shook his head, glancing around for exits one more time. "But he didn't finish testing it. Man, we created an *invasive species* that can live inside our bodies. Remember when all those pythons got into the Everglades? Remember how it fucked up the alligators? This time *we're* the alligators, and we've got somebody's pet store python slithering around inside us. And we don't know what it eats, and we don't know how big it's going to get."

"What are you saying?"

83

Matt looked at Robert Stalnaker, and smiled a bitter death's-head grin as he said, "I'm saying that we're screwed, Mr. Stalnaker, and I'm saying that it's all your fucking fault."

—

The trial of Brandon Majors and Hazel Allen, the ringleaders of the so-called "Mayday Army," has been delayed indefinitely while the precise extent of their crimes is determined. Breaking and entering and willful destruction of property are easy; the sudden demand by the World Health Organization that they also be charged with biological terrorism and global pollution is somewhat more complex...

July 17, 2014: Atlanta, Georgia.

We have a problem."

Ian Matras looked up from his computer screen and blanched, barely recognizing his colleague. Chris looked like he'd managed to lose fifteen pounds in five days. His complexion was waxen, and the circles under his eyes were almost dark enough to make it seem like he'd been punched. "Christ, Chris, what the hell happened to you?"

"The Kellis cure." Chris Sinclair shook his head, rubbing one stubbly cheek as he said, "I don't have it. I mean, I don't think. We still can't test for it, and we can't afford to have me get sick right now just to find out. But the Kellis cure is what happened. It's what's happening right now."

"What are you talking about?"

"There's been a development in one of the research studies we've been monitoring."

85

"The McKenzie-Beatts TB treatment." It wasn't a question, because it didn't need to be. Ian was abruptly glad that he hadn't bothered to stand. He would have just fallen back into his chair.

"Got it in one." Chris nodded, expression grim. "The patients involved in the trial died, Ian. Every one of them."

"When?"

"About an hour and a half ago. Dr. Li was on-site to monitor their symptoms. The first to start seizing was a twenty-seven-year-old male. He began bleeding from the mouth, eyes, nose, and rectum; when they performed the autopsy, they found that he was also bleeding internally, most heavily into his intestines and lungs. It's a coin-toss whether he suffocated or bled out." Chris looked away, toward the blank white wall. He'd never wanted to see the ocean so badly in his life. "The rest started seizing within fifteen minutes. An eleven-year-old girl who'd been accepted into the trials a week before the Kellis cure was released was the last to die. Dr. Li says she was asking for her parents right up until she stopped breathing."

"Oh my God..." whispered Ian.

"I'm telling you, man, I don't think he's here." Chris rubbed his cheek again, hard. "You ready for the bad part?"

Numbly, Ian asked, "You mean that *wasn't* the bad part?"

"Not by a long shot." Chris laughed darkly. "Everyone who had direct contact with the patients—the medical staff, their families, hell, *our* medical staff—has started to experience increased salivation, even though the trial virus was certified as non-contagious. Whatever this stuff is turning into, it's catching. They're sealing the building. Dr. Li's called for an L-4 quarantine. If they don't figure out what's going on, they're going to die in there."

Ian said nothing.

"The malaria folks? We don't know what's going on there. They stopped transmitting an hour before the complex blew sky-high. From what little we've been able to piece together, the charges were set inside the main lab. They, too, decided that they needed a strict quarantine. They just wanted to be absolutely sure that no one was going to have the chance to break it."

There was still a piece missing. Slowly, almost terrified of what the answer would be—no, not almost; *absolutely* terrified of what the answer would be—Ian asked, "What about the Marburg trials in Colorado?"

"They're all fine."

Ian stared at him. "What? But you said—"

"It was spreading, and it was. As far as I know, it still is. Half of Denver's had a nosebleed they couldn't stop. And nobody's died. The bleeding lasts three days, and then it clears up on its own, and the victims feel better than they've felt in years. We have a contagious cure for cancer to go with our contagious cure for the common cold." Chris laughed again. This time, there was a sharp edge of hysteria under the sound. "It's not going to end there. We don't get this lucky. We *can't* get this lucky."

"Maybe this is as bad as it gets." Ian knew how bad the words sounded as soon as they left his mouth, but he couldn't call them back, and he wouldn't have done it even if he could. Someone had to calm Cassandra when she predicted the fall of Troy. Someone had to say "the symptoms aren't that bad" when the predictions called for the fall of man.

Chris gave him a withering look. "Say that like you mean it, or I'm going home to Santa Cruz."

He couldn't, and so he said nothing at all, and the two of them looked at each other, waiting for the end of the world.

—

The CDC has no comment on the tragic deaths in San Antonio, Texas. Drs. Lauren McKenzie and Taylor Beatts were conducting a series of clinical trials aimed at combating drug-resistant strains of tuberculosis...

July 18, 2014: The Rising.

t began nowhere. It began everywhere. It began without warning; it began with all the warning in the world. It could have been prevented a thousand times over. There was nothing that anyone could have done.

It began on July 18th, 2014.

At 6:42 AM, EST, in a hotel in Columbus, Ohio, Lauren Morris rolled over in her sleep and sighed. That was all; the starting bell of the apocalypse was a simple exhale by a sleeping woman unaware of the transformation going on inside her body. Marburg Amberlee and the Kellis cure fell dormant as their children, their beautiful, terrible children, swarmed through Lauren's blood and into her organs, taking over every function and claiming every nerve. At 6:48 AM, Lauren's body opened its eyes, and the virus looked out upon the world, and found that it was hungry. She would be found clawing at the door three hours later when the maids came to clean her room. The room did not get cleaned.

At 9:53 AM, CDT, in the city of Peoria, Illinois, Michael Dowell was hit by a car while crossing the street at a busy intersection. Despite flying more than three yards through the air and hitting the ground with a bone-shattering degree of force, Michael climbed back to his feet almost immediately, to the great relief of bystanders and drivers alike. This relief turned quickly to bewilderment and terror as he lunged at the crowd, biting four people before he could be subdued.

At 10:15 AM, PDT, in the town of Lodi, California, Debbie Goldman left her home and began jogging along her usual route, despite the already record-breaking heat and the recent warnings of her physician. Her explosive cardiac event struck at 11:03 AM. Death was almost instantaneous. Her collapse went unwitnessed, as did her subsequent revival. She staggered to her feet, no longer moving at anything resembling a jog. As she made her way along the road, she encountered a group of teenagers walking to the neighborhood AM/PM; three of the six were bitten in the struggle which followed.

At 11:31 AM, MDT, at the Colorado Cancer Research Center in Denver, Colorado, two of the patients from the Marburg Amberlee cancer trials went into spontaneous viral amplification as the live viral bodies already active in their systems were pushed into a form of slumber by the encroaching Kellis-Amberlee infection. The primary physician's administrative assistant, Janice Barton, was

Countdown

able to trigger the alarm before she was overtaken by the infected. The details of this outbreak remain almost entirely unknown, as the lab was successfully sealed and burned to the ground before the infection could spread.

Ironically, Denver was the source point for one of the two viruses responsible for ending the world, and yet it was spared the worst ravages of the Rising until the second wave began on July 26th. Some say that the tragedy which followed came about only because of that temporary reprieve; they weren't prepared. Those people are not entirely wrong.

And so it went, over and over, all throughout North America. Some of the infected suffered nosebleeds before amplification began, signaling an elevated level of the Marburg Amberlee virus; others did not. Some of the infected would find themselves trapped in cars or hotel rooms, thwarted by stairs or doorknobs; others would not. The Rising had begun.

At 6:18 AM, GMT, on July 19th, in the city of London, England, Lawrence Whitaker was waiting for the Central Line Tube to arrive and take him to work when he felt a warm wetness on his upper lip. He touched it lightly, and frowned at the blood covering his fingertips. He hadn't had a nosebleed since he was a boy. Then he shrugged, produced a tissue, and wiped the blood away. Nothing to be done.

At 3:47 PM, IST, in the city of Mumbai, India, Sanjiv Gupta was answering calls for the American company whose customers he supported when he realized

91

that his eyes were no longer quite focusing on the screen. Pleading exhaustion, he excused himself for his afternoon break, retreating to the employee restroom. He rinsed his eyes three times, but the blurriness in his vision didn't go away. Then his nose began to bleed, and an inability to see became the least of his problems.

And so it went, over and over, all throughout the world. The end was beginning at last.

—

Reports of unusually violent behavior are coming in from across the Midwest, leading some to speculate that the little brown bat, which has been known to migrate during warm weather, may have triggered a rabies epidemic of previously unseen scope...

July 19, 2014: Berkeley, California.

In looking at the biological structure of the screw-fly, the real question isn't 'What was evolution thinking,' it's 'Are any of you paying attention to me, or should I just stop talking and put all of this on your final exam'?" Professor Michael Mason picked up one of the books on his desk and dropped it without ceremony. The resulting boom made half the students jump, and made almost all of them guiltily focus their attention on the front of the lecture hall. Michael folded his arms. "Since you're all clearly sharing with the rest of the class, does anybody feel like sharing with *me*?"

Silence fell over the lecture hall. Michael cocked his head slightly to the side, watching them, and waited. Finally, one of the students cleared her throat and said, "It's just there are these crazy stories going around campus, you know? So we're a little on-edge."

"Crazy stories? Crazy stories like what?"

One of the football players who was taking the class for science credit said, "Like dead dudes getting up and walking around and eating living dudes."

"We're living in a Romero movie!" shouted someone at the back of the room, drawing nervous laughter from the rest of the students.

"All right, now, settle down. Let's approach this like scientists—if it's important enough to distract you all from the important business of biology, we should do it the honor of thinking about it like rational people. You mentioned Romero movies. Does that mean you're positing zombies?"

There was another flurry of laughter. It ended quickly, replaced by dead seriousness. "I think we are, Professor," said the herpetology major in the front row. She shook her head. "It's the only thing that makes sense."

Another student rolled his eyes. "Because zombies *always* make sense."

She glared at him. "Shut up."

"Make me."

"Now that we have demonstrated once again that no human being is ever more than a few steps away from pulling pigtails on the playground, who wants to posit a reason that we'd have zombies now, rather than, oh, six weeks ago?" Michael looked around the room. "Come on. I'm playing along with you. Now one of you needs to play along with me."

"That Mayday Army thing." The words came from a tiny biochem major who almost never spoke during class;

Countdown

she just sat there taking notes with a single-minded dedication that was more frightening than admirable. It was like she thought the bottom of the bell curve would be shot after every exam. She wasn't taking notes now. She was looking at Professor Mason with wide, serious eyes, pencil finally down. "They released an experimental, genetically engineered pathogen into the atmosphere. Dr. Kellis hadn't reached human trials yet. If there were going to be side effects, he didn't have time to find out what they were."

She sounded utterly serene, like she'd finally found a test that she was certain she could pass. Michael Mason paused. "That's an interesting theory, Michelle."

"The CDC has shut down half a dozen clinical trials in the last week, and they won't say why," she replied, as if that had some bearing on the conversation.

Maybe it did. Michael Mason straightened. "All right. I'm going to humor you, because it's not every day that one gets a zombie apocalypse as an excuse for canceling class. You're all dismissed, on one condition."

"What's that, Professor?" asked a student.

"I want you all to stay together. Check your phones for news; check your Twitter feeds. See if anything strange is going on before you go anywhere." He forced a smile, wishing he wasn't starting to feel so uneasy. "If we're having a zombie apocalypse, let's make it a minor one, and all be back here on Monday, all right?"

Laughter and applause greeted his words. He stayed at the front of the room until the last of the students had streamed out; then he grabbed his coat and started for the exit himself. He needed to cancel classes for the rest of the day. He needed to call Stacy and tell her to get Phillip from his kindergarten. If there was one thing science had taught him, it was that safe was always better than sorry, and some things were never on the final exam.

—

Professor Michael Mason has announced the cancellation of class for the rest of the week. His podcast will be posted tomorrow night, as scheduled. All students are given a one-week extension on their summer term papers.

July 20, 2014: Manhattan, New York.

The anchorman had built his reputation on looking sleek and well-groomed even when broadcasting from the middle of a hurricane. His smile was a carefully honed weapon of reassurance, meant to be deployed when bad news might otherwise whip the populace into a frenzy. He was smiling steadily. He had been smiling since the beginning of his report.

He was beginning to wonder if he would ever stop smiling again.

"Again, ladies and gentlemen, there is nothing to be concerned about. We have two particularly virulent strains of flu sweeping across the country. One, in the Midwest, seems to be a variant of our old friend, H1N1, coming back to get revenge for all those bacon, lettuce, and tomato sandwiches. Symptoms include nausea, dizziness, disorientation, and of course, our old friend, the stuffy nose. This particular flu also carries a risk of high fevers, which can lead to erratic behavior and even violence. So please, take care of yourself and your loved ones."

He shuffled the papers in front of him, trying to give the impression that he was reading off them and not off the prompter. Audiences liked to see a little hard copy. It made them feel like the news was more legitimate. "The second strain is milder but a bit more alarming. Thus far, it's stayed on the West Coast—maybe it likes the beach. This one doesn't involve high fevers, for which we can all be grateful, but it does include some pretty nasty nosebleeds, and those can make people seem a lot sicker than they really are. If your nose starts bleeding, simply grab a tissue and head for your local hospital. They'll be able to fix you right up."

He was still smiling. He was never going to not be smiling. He was going to *die* smiling. He knew it, and still the news rolled on. "Now, ladies and gentlemen, I have to beg you to indulge me for a moment. Some individuals are trying to spin this as a global pandemic, and I wish to assure you that it is nothing more than a nasty pair of summer flus. Please do not listen to reports from unreliable sources. Stick with the news outlets that have served you well, and remember, we're here to make sure you know the *real* story."

"And…we're clear!" said one of the production assistants, as the cheery strains of the station break music began to play. The anchor kept smiling. "Great job, Dave. You're doing fantastic. Can I get you anything?"

Countdown

"I'm good," said the anchor, and kept smiling. No one seemed to have noticed that they had no footage, no reports from experts or comments from the man on the street. All they had was a press release from the governor's office and strict orders to read it as written, with no deviation or side commentary. They were being managed, and no one seemed to care, and so he kept on smiling and waited for the commercial break to end.

There was no footage. There was *always* footage. Even when good taste and human decency said not to air it, there was footage. Humanity liked to slow down and look at the car crash by the side of the road, and it was the job of the news to give them all the wrecks that they could stomach. So where was the wreck? Where was the twisted metal and the sorrowful human interest story? Why did they have nothing but words on a teleprompter and silence from the editing room?

"And we're back in five...four...three..." The production assistant stopped in mid-countdown, eyes going terribly wide. "Dave? Do you feel all right?"

"I'm fine. Why?" He kept smiling.

"You're bleeding."

The news anchor—Dave Ramsey, who had done his job, and done it well, for fifteen years—became suddenly aware of a warm wetness on his upper lip. He raised his fingers to touch it, and looked wide-eyed at the blood covering them when he pulled away again. His smile didn't falter. "Oh," he said. "Perhaps I should go clean up."

When the broadcast resumed, his co-anchor was sitting there, a cheerful smile on her face. "We have an update from the Centers for Disease Control, who want us to reassure you that a vaccine will be available soon—"

—

News anchor Dave Ramsey passed away last night of complications from a sudden illness. He was forty-eight years old. A fifteen-year veteran of Channel 51, Dave Ramsey is survived by his wife and three children...

July 26, 2014: Denver, Colorado.

S uzanne Amberlee's nose had been bleeding for most of the morning. It had ceased to bother her after the first hour; in a way, it had even proven itself a blessing. The blood loss seemed to blunt the hard edges of the world around her, blurring things into a comfortable gray that allowed her to finally face some of the hard tasks she'd been allowing herself to avoid. She paused in the process of boxing Amanda's books, wiping the sweat from her forehead with one hand and the blood from her chin with the other. Bloody handprints marred every box and wall in the room, but she didn't really see them anymore. She just saw the bitter absence of Amanda, who was never coming home to her again.

In Suzanne Amberlee's body, a battle was raging between the remaining traces of Marburg Amberlee and the newborn Kellis-Amberlee virus. There is no loyalty among viruses; as soon as they were fully conceived, the child virus turned against its parents, trying to drive them from the body as it would any other infection. This forced the Marburg into a heightened state of activity, which forced the body to respond to the perceived illness. Marburg Amberlee was not designed to fight the human body's immune system, and responded by launching a full-on assault. The resulting chaos was tearing Suzanne apart from the inside out.

For her part, Suzanne Amberlee neither knew nor cared about what was happening inside her body. She was one of the first to be infected with Marburg Amberlee, which had been tailored to be non-transmissible between humans...but nothing's perfect, and all those kisses she'd given her little girl had, in time, passed something more tangible than comfort between them. Marburg Amberlee had had plenty of time to establish itself inside her, and, paradoxically, that made her more resistant to conversion than those with more recent infections. Her body knew how to handle the sleeping virus.

And yet bit by bit, inch by crucial inch, Kellis-Amberlee was winning. Suzanne was not aware, but she was already losing crucial brain functions. Her tear ducts had ceased to function, and much of her body's moisture was being channeled toward the production of mucus and saliva—two reliable mechanisms for passing the infection along. She was being rewired, inch by inch and cell by cell, and even if someone had explained to her what was happening, she wouldn't have cared.

Countdown

Suzanne Amberlee had lost everything she ever loved. Losing herself was simply giving in to the inevitable.

Suzanne's last conscious thought was of her daughter, and how much she missed her. Then the stuffed bear she was holding slipped from her hands, and all thoughts slipped from her mind as she straightened and walked toward the open bedroom door. The back door was propped open, allowing a cool breeze to blow in from outside; she walked through it, and from there, made her way out of the backyard to the street.

The disaster that had been averted when the Colorado Cancer Research Center burned began with a woman, widowed and bereft of her only child, walking barefoot onto the sun-baked surface of the road. She looked dully to either side, not really tracking what she saw—not by any human definition of the term—before turning to walk toward the distant shouts of children playing in the neighborhood park. It would take her the better part of an hour to get there, moving slowly, with the jerky confusion of the infected when not actively pursuing visible prey.

It would take less than ten minutes after her arrival for the dying to begin. The Rising had come to Denver; the Rising had come home.

—

Please return to your homes. Please remain calm. This is not a drill. If you have been infected, please contact

Countdown

authorities immediately. If you have not been infected, please remain calm. This is not a drill. Please return to your homes...

July 26, 2014:
Allentown, Pennsylvania.

The people outside the prison could pretend that the dead weren't walking if they wanted to. That sort of bullshit was the province of the free. Once you were behind bars, counting on other people to bring you food, water, hell, to let you go to the bathroom like a human being...you couldn't lie to yourself. And the dead *were* walking.

So far, there hadn't been any outbreaks in Brandon's wing of the prison, but he knew better than to attribute that to anything beyond pure dumb luck. Whatever caused some people to get sick and die and then get up again without being bitten just hadn't found a way inside the building. It would. All it needed was a little more time, and it would.

Brandon was sitting on his bed and staring at his hands, wondering if he'd ever see Hazel again, when the door of his cell slid open. He raised his head, and found himself looking at one of the prison guards—one of the only guards who was still bothering to show up for work.

"You've got a visitor, Majors," said the guard, and gestured roughly for him to stand. Brandon had learned the virtue of obedience. It was practically the first lesson that prison taught. He stood, moving quickly to avoid a reprimand.

There had been other lessons since then. None of them had been pleasant ones.

The guard led Brandon through the halls without a word. Some of the prisoners shouted threats or profanity as they passed; Brandon's role in the Mayday Army was well-known, and was the reason he was placed in solitary. As the situation got worse, his future looked more and more bleak. Outside the prison, he would probably have already been lynched. As if it was his fault somehow? That bastard Kellis was the one who built the bug. He should be the one getting the blame, not Brandon—

The guard led him around the corner to the visiting room. There were only two men standing there. One was the warden. The other was a slim, dark-haired man Brandon felt like he should recognize. Something about him was familiar.

"Brandon Majors?" asked the man.

"Yes?" Maybe he was from the governor. Maybe he had come to pardon Brandon and take him away from all this; maybe he understood that it wasn't his fault—

"My name is Alexander Kellis."

Hope died. Brandon stared at him. "I…you…oh, God."

Countdown

Alexander looked at Brandon—the little ringleader who had managed to bring about the end of the world, the one whose name was already dropping out of the news, to be replaced by Alexander's own—and said, very quietly, "I wanted to meet you. I wanted to look you in the eye while I told you that this is all your fault. History may blame it on me, but neither of us is going to be there to see it, and right here, right now, today, this is all your fault. You destroyed my life's work. You killed the man I loved. You may very well have brought about the end of the world. So I have just one question for you."

"What?" whispered Brandon.

"Was it worth it?" After five minutes passed with no answer, Dr. Kellis turned to the warden. "Thank you. I'd like to go now." They walked away, leaving Brandon standing frozen next to the guard.

That night, Brandon's cell was somehow left unlocked. He was found dead in the hall the next morning, having been stabbed more than a dozen times. None of the other inmates saw what happened. At least, that's what they said, and this one time, the warden chose to believe them. It wasn't his fault, after all.

—

If you have not been infected, please remain calm. This is not a drill. Please return to your homes. Please remain calm. This is not a drill. If you have been infected, please contact authorities immediately...

July 27, 2014: Berkeley, California.

"Get those walls up! Cathy, I want to see that chicken wire hugging those planks, don't argue with me, just *get it done.*" Stacy Mason rushed to help a group of neighborhood teens who staggered under the weight of the planks they'd "liberated" from an undisclosed location. At this point, she didn't care where the building materials came from; she cared only that they were going to reinforce the neighborhood fences and doors and road checkpoints. As long as what was inside their makeshift walls was going to make those walls stronger, they could start tearing down houses and she honestly wouldn't give a fuck.

Berkeley, being a university town in Northern California, had two major problems: not enough guns, and too many idiots who thought they could fight off zombies with medieval weapons they'd stolen from the history department. It also had two major advantages:

111

most of the roads were already half-blocked to prevent campus traffic from disturbing the residents, and most of those residents were slightly insane by any normal societal measurement.

The nice lesbian collective down the block had contributed eighty feet of chicken wire left over from an urban farming project they'd managed the year before. The robotics engineer who lived across the street was an avid Burner, and had been happy to contribute the fire-breathing whale he'd constructed for the previous year's Burning Man. Not the most immediately useful contribution in the world, but it was sufficiently heavy to make an excellent road block…and Stacy had to admit that having a fire-breathing road block certainly gave the neighborhood character.

"Louise! If you're going to break the glass, break it clean—we don't want anyone getting cut!" They really, *really* didn't want anyone getting cut. The transmission mechanisms for the zombie virus were still being charted, but fluid exchange was definitely on the list, and anything getting into an open wound seemed like a bad idea. "We gave you a hammer for a reason! Now *smash* things!"

The distant shrieks of children brought her head whipping around, the hairs on the back of her neck standing on end. Then the shrieks mellowed into laughter, and she relaxed—not entirely, but enough. "Damn dogs," she muttered, a smile tugging at her lips. "Exciting the children and stopping my heart."

Countdown

"Mrs. Mason? I can't figure out how to make the staple gun work." The plaintive cry came from a young woman who had been Phillip's babysitter several times over the summer. She was standing next to a sheet of plywood with a staple gun in her hand, shaking it helplessly. It wasn't spewing staples at the moment; a small mercy, since the last thing they needed was for everyone to get hit by friendly fire.

Stacy shook off her brief fugue, starting toward the girl. "That's because you're holding it wrong, Marie. Now please, point the staple gun *away* from your body..."

The comfortable chaos of a neighborhood protecting itself against the dangerous outside continued, with everyone doing the best that they could to shore up their defenses and walls. They'd lost people on supply runs and rescue trips, but so far everyone who'd stayed on the block had been fine. They were clinging to that, as the power got intermittent and the supply runs got less fruitful. Help was coming. Help had to be coming. And when help arrived, it would find them ready, healthy, and waiting to be saved.

Stacy Mason might be living through the zombie apocalypse, but by God, the important word there was "living." She was going to make it through, and so was everyone she cared about. There was just no other way that this could end.

—

MIRA GRANT

If you are receiving this broadcast, you are within the range of the UC Berkeley radio station. Please follow these directions to reach a safe location. You will be expected to surrender all weapons and disrobe for physical examination upon arrival. We have food. We have water. We have shelter...

July 27, 2014: Denver, Colorado.

Denver was burning. From where Dr. Wells sat, in the front room of his mountain home, it looked like the entire city was on fire. That couldn't possibly be true—Denver was too large to burn that easily—but oh, it looked that way.

In the house behind him he could hear the sound of shuffling, uncertain footsteps as his wife and children made their way down the stairs to the hallway. He didn't move. Not even to shut the door connecting the living room with the rest of the house. He was lonely. His city was burning, his research was over, and he was lonely. Couldn't a man be lonely, when he was sitting at the end of the world and watching Denver burn?

Daniel Wells lifted his scotch, took a sip, and lowered it again. His eyes never left the flames. They were alive. Even if nothing else in the city he called home was alive, the flames were thriving. There was something comforting in that. Life, as a wise man once said, would always find a way.

A low moan sounded from the hallway right outside the front room. Daniel took another sip of scotch. "Hello, darling," he said, without turning. "It's a beautiful day, don't you think? All this smoke is going to make for an amazing sunset..."

Then his wife and children, who had finished amplification some time before, fell upon him, and the man responsible for Marburg Amberlee knew nothing but the tearing of teeth and the quiet surrender to the dark. When he opened his eyes again, he wasn't Daniel Wells anymore. Had he still possessed the capacity for gratitude, it is very likely that he would have been grateful.

—

This is not a drill. If you have been infected, please contact authorities immediately. If you have not been infected, please remain calm. This is not a drill. Please return to your homes. Please remain calm. This is not a drill...

July 30, 2014: Reston, Virginia.

t had taken six of the Valium pills John kept hidden at the back of the medicine cabinet, but Alexander Kellis was finally ready. He checked the knot on his rope one more time. It was good; it would hold. Maybe it wasn't elegant, but he didn't deserve elegant, did he? He destroyed the world. Children would curse his name for generations, assuming there were any generations to come. John was gone, forever. It was over.

"I'll see you soon, sweetheart," he whispered, and stepped off the edge of his desk. No one would find his body for weeks. If he reanimated, he starved without harming anyone. Alexander Kellis never harmed anyone.

Not on purpose.

—

Please return to your homes. Please remain calm. This is not a drill. If you have been infected, please contact authorities immediately. If you have not been infected, please remain calm. This is not a drill. Please return to your homes...

July 30, 2014: Atlanta, Georgia.

The bedroom walls were painted a cheery shade of rose petal pink that showed up almost neon in the lens of the web camera. Unicorns and rainbows decorated the page where the video was embedded; even the YouTube mirrors that quickly started appearing had unicorns and rainbows, providing a set of safe search words that were too widespread to be wiped off the internet, no matter how many copies of the video were taken down. The man sitting in front of the web cam was all wrong for the blog. Too old, too haggard, too afraid. His once-pristine lab coat was spattered with coffee stains, and he looked like he hadn't shaved in more than a week.

"My name is Dr. Ian Matras," he said, in a calm, clear voice that was entirely at odds with his appearance. "I am—I was; I suppose I'm not anymore—an epidemic researcher for the Centers for Disease Control. I have been working on the issue of the Kellis cure since it was first allowed into the atmosphere. I have been tracking the development of the epidemic, along with my colleague, Dr. Christopher Sinclair." His breath hitched, voice threatening to break. He got himself back under control, and continued, "Chris wouldn't sanction what I'm going to say next. Good thing he isn't around to tell me not to say it, right?

"The news has been lying to you. This is not a virulent summer cold; this is not a new strain of the swine flu. This is, and has always been, a man-made pandemic whose effects were previously unknown in higher mammals. Put bluntly, the Kellis cure has mutated, becoming conjoined with an experimental Marburg-based cure for cancer. It is airborne. It is highly contagious. And it raises the dead.

"Almost everyone who breathes air is now infected with this virus. Transmission is apparently universal, and does not come with any initial symptoms. The virus will change forms under certain conditions, going from the passive 'helper' form to the active 'killer' form of what we've been calling Kellis-Amberlee. Once this process begins, there is nothing that can stop it. Anyone whose virus has begun to change forms is going to become one of the mindless cannibals now shambling around our streets. Why? We don't know. What we do know is that fluid transmission seems to trigger the active form of the virus—bites, scratches, even getting something in your eye. Some people may seroconvert spontaneously.

Countdown

We believe these people were involved with the Marburg trials in Colorado, but following the destruction of the facility where those trials were conducted, we have no way of being absolutely sure.

"Let me repeat: we have been lying to you. The government is not allowing us to spread any knowledge about the walking plague, saying that we would trigger a mass panic. Well, the masses are panicking, and I don't think keeping secrets is doing anybody any favors. Not at this stage.

"Once someone has converted into the...hell, once somebody's a zombie, there's no coming back. They are no longer the people you have known all your life. Head shots seem to work best. Severe damage to the body will eventually cause them to bleed out, but it can take time, and it will create a massive hot zone that can't be sterilized with anything but fire or bleach. We have... God, we have..." He stopped for a moment, dropping his forehead into the palm of his hand. Finally, dully, he said, "We have lied to you We have withheld information. What follows is everything we know about this disease, and the simple fact of it is, we know there isn't any cure. We know we can't stop it.

"Early signs of amplification include dilated pupils, blurred vision, dry mouth, difficulty breathing, loss of coordination, unexplained mood swings, personality changes, apparent lapses in memory, aphasia..."

—

If you have been infected, please contact authorities immediately. If you have not been infected, please remain calm. This is not a drill. Please return to your homes. Please remain calm. This is not a drill. If you have been infected...

July 31, 2014: Berkeley, California.

Marigold felt bad.

There had been a raccoon in the yard. She liked when raccoons came to the yard, they puffed up big so big, but they ran ran ran when you chased them, and the noises they made were like birds or squirrels but bigger and more exhilarating. She had chased the raccoon, but the raccoon didn't run. Instead, it held its ground, and when she came close enough, it bit her on the shoulder, hard, teeth tearing skin and flesh and leaving only pain pain pain behind. Then she ran, *she* ran from the raccoon, and she had rolled in the dirt until the bleeding stopped, mud clotting the wound, pain pain pain muted a little behind the haze of her confusion. Then had come shame. Shame, because she would be called bad dog for chasing raccoons; bad dog for getting bitten when there were so many people in the house and yard and everything was strange.

So Marigold did what any good dog in fear of being termed a bad dog would do; she had gone to the hole in the back of the fence, the hole she and her brother worked and worried so long at, and slunk into the yard next door, where the boy lived. The boy laughed and pulled her ears sometimes, but it never hurt. The boy loved her. She knew the boy loved her, even as she knew that the man and the woman fed her and that she was a good dog, really, all the way to the heart of her. She was a good dog.

She was a good dog, but she felt so bad. So very bad. The badness had started with the bite, but it had spread since then, and now she could barely swallow, and the light was hurting her eyes so much, so very much. She lay huddled under the bushes, wishing she could find her feet, wishing she knew why she felt bad. So very bad.

Marigold felt hungry.

The hunger was a new thing, a strong thing, stronger even than the bad feeling that was spreading through her. She considered the hunger, as much as she could. She had never been the smartest of dogs, and her mind was getting fuzzy, thought and impulse giving way to alien instinct. She was a good dog. She just felt bad. She was a good dog. She was...she was...she was hungry. Marigold was hungry. Then she was only hunger, and no more Marigold. No more Marigold at all.

Something rustled through the bushes. The dog that had been a good dog, that had been Marigold, and that was now just hungry, rose slowly, legs unsteady but willing to support the body if there might be something coming

124

that could end the hunger. The dog that had been a good dog, that had been Marigold, looked without recognition at the figure that parted the greenery and peered down at it with wide-eyed curiosity. The dog, which had always been ready with a welcoming bark, made a sound that was close to a moan.

"Oggie?"

—

We are experiencing technical difficulties. Please stand by.

August 1, 2014.

Kellis-Amberlee unified the world in a way that nothing had ever unified it before, or ever would again. Cities burned. Nations died. Tokyo, Manhattan, Mumbai, London, all of them fell before an enemy that could not be stopped, because it came from within; because it was already inside. Some escaped. Some lived. All carried the infection deep inside their bodies, tucked away where it could never be excised. They carried it with them, and it lived, too.

The Rising was finally, fully underway. Mothers mourned their children. Orphans wailed alone in the night. Death ruled over all, horrible and undying. And nothing, it seemed, would ever make it end.

But on the internet, Dr. Matras's message repeated, over and over again, and others began repeating it with him. The future was arriving. All they had to do was live to see it. So the world asked itself a question:

When will you Rise?
And the world gave itself an answer:
Now.
Welcome to the aftermath.

—

"In telling the stories of the Rising, we must remember this above all else: we did what everyone claimed mankind could never do. We survived. Now it is up to us to prove that we deserved this second chance." –Mahir Gowda

APOCALYPSE SCENARIO NO. 683: THE BOX

∞

Andy, where's the beer?"

"Look in the crisper."

Ryan paused before asking the obvious: "Why is the beer in the crisper?"

"Because grain's a vegetable," said Elsa, sensibly enough, as she dumped tortilla chips into a yellow plastic bowl. "That means beer is good for you."

"I don't even know what to say to that," said Ryan, before digging a beer out from under a wilted head of lettuce. "Is Mike coming?"

"Mike's coming, Cole isn't." Andy picked up the tray of sandwiches, pausing to kiss Elsa on the cheek before exiting the kitchen. The tray of sandwiches was placed ceremoniously on the dining room table, next to a veggie platter, a bowl of salsa, and a second bowl filled with peanut M&Ms. He glanced back as Ryan followed him to the table, adding, "Before you ask, Sandi's coming. She just had to stop and pick up some root beer."

"Right." Ryan sat in his usual chair, cracking open his first beer of the evening. He'd stop after the third, when

Sandi's nagging became too much for him to handle. None of this was a mystery to anyone, and that was how all of them liked it. Playing the Apocalypse Game for fifteen years had transformed predictability into one of the weekly game night's greatest attractions. Spend some time with your friends, play a board game you didn't really care about, and plot the downfall of mankind. Pure bliss.

Cole's absence was the only black spot on what was otherwise shaping up to be a perfect evening. She'd been more and more scarce over the past few years, as her job—which she never described in detail, being willing to say nothing beyond "I work for the government" and "I still use my medical degree"—kept her away from home more and more often. Even saying that much made her visibly uncomfortable, until they all stopped asking.

Still, Cole missing the Apocalypse Game was still a new phenomenon—new enough to be unnerving. Out of all the players, she'd always been the most reliable. "Remember the time Cole had pneumonia?" asked Ryan. "She missed two sessions in a row."

"And then she showed up for the third session in her bathrobe." Andy laughed, shaking his head. "Mike was so disappointed when he realized she had her clothes on underneath it."

"Those were the days." Ryan took a long swig from his beer, amusement fading. "This is the third session. She's never missed three."

"There's a first time for everything."

Apocalypse Scenario No. 683: The Box

"I'm worried about her," said Elsa, emerging from the kitchen with the bowl of chips in her hands. "She's been working too much. She needs the Apocalypse Game to take her mind off things."

Ryan snorted. "I'm going to give you a second to think about what you just said."

"I stand by it. Cole started the Game. She should be able to find the time to play."

"I'm sure she'll be back as soon as she can," said Andy.

"I hope so." Elsa sighed. "Maybe Mike can tell us more."

"Maybe," Andy agreed dolefully. Silence descended.

Their little social group was just like a thousand others, all over the world, at least superficially: a bunch of old friends getting together to play games and talk until well after any sensible person's bedtime. They met in high school, a bunch of strange, smart kids living on the fringes of teenage society. They clustered together in self-defense, as much as anything else—it wasn't until midway through freshman year that they all started to actually like each other.

The first Apocalypse Game was practically an accident. They'd been lazing around Cole's house, bored and restless and looking for something to do. They'd tried everything from Poker to Candyland before Cole made her characteristically mild suggestion: "Why don't we figure out how to destroy the world?"

The first scenario was Cole's of course. It involved a chemical spill wiping out the world's plankton supply.

Without plankton, the small fish died; without the small fish, the big fish died; without the big fish, everything else in the ocean followed suit. It was an ineffective, inelegant apocalypse, and after they'd spent the whole night debating it, Ryan said he could do better. Elsa dared him to prove it. A week later, he did. Sandi took the week after that, and so on, and so on. High school ended. College began. Dan and Tony moved away; Elsa and Andy got married; Cole and Mike didn't, although they may as well have. And always, always, there was the Game.

Maybe it was a strange way to spend fifteen years of Friday nights. At the end of the day, none of them really cared.

—

The five players took their seats around the dining room table. The chair next to Mike remained conspicuously empty. None of them could avoid glancing at it at least once. Cole's absence was palpable, and it couldn't be ignored, no matter how hard everyone tried. She should have been there.

Mike cleared his throat. "I, uh, brought something. Well, Cole sent something."

"Behind her love, her regrets, and a promise that she'll do her best to make it next week?" asked Sandi, reaching for her second root beer.

"If you run out, we're not stopping so you can go for more," cautioned Andy.

Apocalypse Scenario No. 683: The Box

Sandi shot him a glare. "I know that."

Elsa raised a hand, stopping the familiar argument before it could begin. "What did she send?"

"Well, Sandi was right about Cole sending her love and her regrets. She also sent this." Mike pulled a small digital recorder from his pocket. He put it down on the table, between the tortilla chips and the veggie platter. "Tonight's supposed to be her turn, right?"

"Right," said Ryan, dubiously. "So what, you're going to present her scenario and record our discussion?"

"No. Cole's presenting her own scenario. I'm here to play the game." Mike pressed the "play" button on the top of the recorder. It beeped, once, before Cole's sweet, always slightly distracted voice came through the speaker, just as clear as if she'd actually been there.

"Hi, guys. I'm sorry I couldn't be there in person tonight, but I had...things...I needed to take care of. This is a scenario I've been working on for a while, and I think it's pretty solid. There will be beeps every few minutes, like this one," the recorder beeped again, "to signal that it's time to pause for discussion before you continue. I think I've predicted all your responses. You could still surprise me."

There was a third beep. Mike leaned forward and paused the recording.

"Well?" he asked. "Is everybody cool with this?"

"It's weird," said Ryan. "Weird is good."

Sandi giggled nervously. "I guess it's okay. I didn't want to skip her turn, anyway."

"Andy? Elsa?"

"I'm cool with it, sure, but do you know what's on the recording?" asked Andy. "Not to be a stickler, but scenarios aren't supposed to be shared before the Game."

"She recorded the whole thing at work and gave it to me before she left for the airport," said Mike. "I'm not a cheater. I didn't listen."

"Then I'm cool with it, too," said Elsa firmly. "Play the scenario."

Mike pressed the button.

—

"If you're listening to this, that means you've decided to let me take my turn. Thank you. I really appreciate it. Anyway, this is Apocalypse Scenario number six hundred and eighty-three. I've never been good with names—I'm more interested in the science—so I just call this scenario 'the Box.'"

"Sounds promising," said Sandi, and took a swig of root beer. Ryan motioned for her to be quiet. She stuck her tongue out at him.

Cole's voice continued implacably: "First, establishment of the scenario. The Box is based around a man-made bacterial pandemic. At the time the scenario begins, the bacteria in question have already been released into the human population at several geographically distinct locations. All the locations were in North America, but

Apocalypse Scenario No. 683: The Box

they all included a very high probability of intercontinental transmission within twenty-four hours, as in Andy's Ticket to Die Apocalypse."

"Cute," said Andy.

"The bacterial strain you're dealing with was designed by a young researcher employed by the bioterrorism division of the United States government. It was originally commissioned under the auspices of 'counterterrorism.'" Cole's voice turned briefly bitter, causing Andy and Elsa to exchange worried glances. Bitterness wasn't native to Cole's state of being. "The people in charge lied about it, of course. That's vital to understanding this scenario: it begins with the assumption that if you reported the scenario to the government, they'd believe you, because the government is the reason the situation exists in the first place."

The recorder beeped. Mike hit the "pause" button and looked around the table. "That's our setup."

"It's pretty simplistic, especially for Cole," said Ryan. "Somebody drops a test tube, somebody else tells the people in charge, and everything gets mopped up with minimal loss of life. The world doesn't end."

"Nobody dropped a test tube," said Elsa. "She said it was released into the human population in 'several geographically diverse locations,' and implied that they were chosen to create the widest possible infection pattern. This thing was intentionally released."

"The government angle still makes it pretty simple," said Andy.

Sandi shrugged. "So it'll be a short apocalypse. Go ahead and press play, Mike. I want to hear what comes next."

Mike nodded, and pressed the button.

The bitterness was gone when Cole resumed her explanation. Instead, she sounded cheerful, if a little overtired. "Second, elaboration of the scenario. You're looking at a bacterial infection based on a combination of whooping cough and tuberculosis—just like Ryan's No Air Apocalypse, only this time, the bacteria has been tailored for antibiotic resistance. The first generation has an artificially long latency built in, to allow for extensive spread. Once the first generations of bacteria have incubated to maturity in human lungs, the latency will be halved, until the final projected generation, where it will default to the standard latency period for whooping cough. Symptoms include coughing, runny nose, headache, difficulty breathing, muscular spasm, secondary pneumonia, and, of course, death.

"Fatality estimates place the death toll at approximately ninety-one percent of the infected population. It's impossible to accurately predict susceptibility, but projections indicate that as much as eighty percent of the human race could be infected by the end of the second latency."

Beep. Pause.

"Okay, that's...charming." Sandi wrinkled her nose. "Has Cole gone off her meds or something? She's not normally this nasty with her scenarios."

Apocalypse Scenario No. 683: The Box

Mike didn't say anything. He reached almost mechanically for the chips, scooping up a handful. His eyes looked haunted. Something about that look frightened Andy in ways he wasn't sure he could put into words. Something was wrong.

"Mike?" he said. "You okay, buddy? Is Cole okay?"

"She's been working a lot lately." Mike forced a laugh. It sounded unnatural enough that Ryan paused with his beer halfway lifted to his mouth. "She's just stressed, that's all. Let's keep going." Mike hit the button before anyone could object, and Cole spoke again.

"Three..." She paused, taking a deep breath. "Three, explanation of apocalypse stemming from scenario. Buckle up, guys. Here's where the real game starts."

—

"See, this researcher, she was recruited right out of college. Her 'scholarship' to medical school wasn't a scholarship, not really; it was a government loan. They'd pay for everything, and she'd go to work for them when she graduated. They wanted her that much, because she was that good." Something like pride crept into Cole's voice. "They knew she'd be able to change the world."

Elsa's hand clamped down on Andy's elbow, squeezing hard. None of them said anything. Every pair of eyes was fixed on the recorder.

"For a while, she was happy with the deal. She thought she was protecting the world against the bad

139

guys—that she could stave off the apocalypse she'd been worrying about since she was in high school. She tore viruses and bacteria apart and recombined them in ways no one else had ever been able to accomplish. She read. She researched. She was going to change the world.

"Only it turned out she already had, because she started hearing about this outbreak in Korea that perfectly mirrored one of her projects—one of her *defensive* projects. People were dying of something that sounded a lot like her enhanced strain of the bubonic plague. She went to her superiors and asked them…asked them if they were going to send help. And they told her to go back to her lab, and get back to work."

"I saw that on the news," whispered Elsa. "So many people died. It was horrible."

Cole continued: "She got scared then, our researcher, and she started really looking at the things she'd been working on. The things that were supposed to help people. Only they weren't helping people at all. They were hurting them. And everyone said that was okay, because we weren't the only ones—every government in the world was doing it, and that made it okay. That made it *necessary*. If we didn't build it, someone else would." She stopped, seeming to lose her place for a moment, before repeating, "Someone else *would*. It wasn't something she could stop by walking away. You know? It was going to happen. We'd made it inevitable. She'd made it inevitable. So maybe the best thing she could do was stop it all before it got even worse. Stop it the only way she knew how. Stop the whole damn arms race for a while, and give everyone a chance to breathe. For certain values of 'everyone,' anyway. Because if she didn't…

"Things have been getting worse for a long time. Everybody knows that. If humanity isn't stopped, they're going to kill the planet, not just themselves. Someone had to do something. She was just the one watching when the time finally came."

Beep; pause.

"This is sick," said Sandi. She popped the cap off her last root beer, glaring at Mike. "Why is she doing this? There's not even anything to discuss. It's just *sick*."

"Mike?" Elsa worried her lip between her teeth for a moment before saying, "Cole never told us who she worked for."

"No." Mike's voice was bleak, empty of all emotion. "She wasn't allowed to. They made her sign a lot of papers."

"A lot of papers in exchange for what?" asked Andy.

"Medical school."

Mike pressed the button.

—

"The release happened six days ago. The infection has a latency of twenty-three days. Additional releases are ongoing. Because…" Cole stopped again before starting back up, sounding more and more like a broken marionette. She was running down. "Because the government funded the original project, they might be able to find a vaccine if they start looking immediately. It wouldn't be hard to type the bacterial strain, and there are only a few researchers working with it. They don't know about all the modifications that I...that she...that were made. They'd need to start right away. But there's a catch."

"Isn't there always?" asked Mike, leaning back in his seat.

"The researcher who created the disease, she's listening in on all the big channels, and a lot of the small ones. She has people feeding her information, people who have really good reason to be loyal to her. People who see the same solution she does. And if she hears a whisper from any government, anywhere, that links this pandemic to her research, she'll release the second project she worked on. The bad one."

"This *isn't* the bad one?" Ryan sounded incredulous. "I mean, come on, Cole..."

"Here's where things get dicey, guys. See, the second virus isn't bacterial. It's a virus, based on a hemorrhagic out of Africa called 'Lassa fever.' It's got a long latency and a high mortality rate, and that's without clever virologists playing with the way it works. And this one hasn't got a vaccine, although it *does* have a nasty little interlock with the vaccine for the bacterial strain. If you would have been immune to the original pandemic, either naturally or due to immunization, you'll get the second virus and you'll die." Cole sighed deeply. "I'm sorry about that."

Apocalypse Scenario No. 683: The Box

"Is she crazy?" demanded Sandi.

"I don't know," said Ryan.

Cole's laughter startled them all, even Mike, who jumped in his chair and nearly knocked over Sandi's root beer. It was a brittle, jagged sound, like broken glass.

"Okay, okay, I give, you guys," she said. "This 'oh, I have a friend' shit is so high school, isn't it? I built the virus. I built them both. The scenario is still valid: the releases started last week. Manhattan, San Francisco, and—best of all—Disney World. I put it in the misters, just like Elsa's Black Fungus Apocalypse. Thanks for that, Elsa. It works great."

Elsa looked ill. Cole kept talking.

"I love you guys. You're the best friends I've ever had. I mean, you may be the only friends I've ever had— the only real ones, anyway. That's why I'm leaving this up to you. I vaccinated you all against the first disease months ago. You're probably the safest people on the planet. Yes, even you, Sandi. I know you slept with Mike, but I don't really care about that anymore. It's too trivial a concern."

Sandi and Mike exchanged a glance, her eyes wide and horrified, his merely resigned. Cole kept talking.

"You're all going to live through what comes next. It won't be fun, but you'll live. I knew you wouldn't want to do it alone—you were always more social than I was—so I've arranged to have a box couriered to Elsa and Andy's place tonight, during the Game. Inside, you'll find ten doses of vaccine for each of you.

Use them however you want. Save your family, or your friends, or your doctor. It's up to you. You can even give them to the government. And if you do, I'll die with you, because I'm immune to the first pandemic, just like you are."

Cole's voice turned wistful. "I wish I could've given you this scenario in person. I think it's the best one I've ever put together. I really wanted to, but in the end, I couldn't risk it. I love you all. I love you all so much. I hope you'll find the answer that's right, because to be honest...I can't. All I can do is end the world, and let you decide how much of it survives.

"This is Cole Evans, signing out." A pause, and then, in a whisper they all had to strain to hear: "Forgive me?"

The recorder beeped one more time. Silence fell.

—

Ryan was the first to react. He laughed nervously, shaking his head. "Okay, wow. That's the best mind-fuck we've had in a while. Points to Cole."

"I don't think she was kidding," said Elsa.

"We haven't answered the scenario yet, guys," said Mike. He picked up the recorder, cradling it in his hand. "Do we call the government and die, or do we condemn millions of people because we're too chicken to pick up the phone?"

"Dude, did you really sleep with Sandi?" asked Ryan.

Mike didn't answer.

Apocalypse Scenario No. 683: The Box

"Won't calling the government mean killing even *more* people?" asked Andy. "She said the second virus was worse."

"We don't know that," said Mike. "Maybe there's only one virus."

"Because Cole was always an underachiever," scoffed Ryan. "If she says there's a second virus in the scenario, there's a second virus in the scenario. I'm just not buying the idea that it's real life."

"Are you willing to risk it?" asked Elsa.

"We're not risking anything," snapped Sandi. "It's a game. It's a stupid game, and that's all it's ever been, and that's all it's ever going to be. Stop taking this so seriously. Cole's just messing with us. That's all."

The doorbell rang.

Silence fell again, thick and heavy as a curtain going down. Elsa looked around the group, meeting everyone's eyes in turn. Then she slowly pushed her chair back from the table, stood, and walked to answer the door.

She was halfway across the room when the person outside began to cough.